Condemned
Marianna Buffolino

Copyright © 2024 by Iannotta Creations Corp.

ALL RIGHTS RESERVED.

No portion of this book may be reproduced in any form without written permission from the publisher or author, except as permitted by U.S. copyright law.

This publication is designed to provide accurate and authoritative information in regard to the subject matter covered. It is sold with the understanding that neither the author nor the publisher is engaged in rendering legal, investment, accounting or other professional services. While the publisher and author have used their best efforts in preparing this book, they make no representations or warranties with respect to the accuracy or completeness of the contents of this book and specifically disclaim any implied warranties of merchantability or fitness for a particular purpose. No warranty may be created or extended by sales representatives or written sales materials. The advice and strategies contained herein may not be suitable for your situation. You should consult with a professional when appropriate. Neither the publisher nor the author shall be liable for any loss of profit or any other commercial damages, including but not limited to special, incidental, consequential, personal, or other damages.

This is a work of fiction. Names, characters, businesses, events, and incidents are the products of the author's imagination. Any resemblance to actual persons, living or dead, or actual events is purely coincidental. This book contains strong language and explicit sexual encounters.

ISBN: 979-8-9897821-1-6

Printed in the United States of America

"A writer is someone who has taught his mind to misbehave."
- Oscar Wilde

Table of Contents

1. Chapter 1 — 1
2. Chapter 2 — 7
3. Chapter 3 — 17
4. Chapter 4 — 20
5. Chapter 5 — 27
6. Chapter 6 — 35
7. Chapter 7 — 42
8. Chapter 8 — 46
9. Chapter 9 — 51
10. Chapter 10 — 57
11. Chapter 11 — 63
12. Chapter 12 — 67
13. Chapter 13 — 73
14. Chapter 14 — 78
15. Chapter 15 — 83
16. Chapter 16 — 90

17.	Chapter 17	94
18.	Chapter 18	98
19.	Chapter 19	105
20.	Chapter 20	109
21.	Chapter 21	116
22.	Chapter 22	122
23.	Chapter 23	125
24.	Chapter 24	130
25.	Chapter 25	135
26.	Chapter 26	139
27.	Chapter 27	146
28.	Chapter 28	157
29.	Chapter 29	160
30.	Chapter 30	165
31.	Chapter 31	170
32.	Chapter 32	173
33.	Chapter 33	178
34.	Chapter 34	183
35.	Chapter 35	191
36.	Chapter 36	197
37.	Chapter 37	201
38.	Chapter 38	208

39.	Chapter 39	213
40.	Chapter 40	217
41.	Chapter 41	223
42.	Chapter 42	228
43.	Chapter 43	234
	Epilogue	237

Chapter 1

The air was thick with passion. Anywhere my vision landed, they fell onto sexual acts played by lovers that varied in participants. Men and women's bodies all over one another sparked this longing of wanting something real—something that made me feel just as alive as these people did living out their fantasies. This was my first time at one of these, and although I was timid, it piqued my curiosity.

"Not what I expected," my boyfriend Casper whispered.

"Well, it is a sex party," giggling as I whispered back.

"I can't believe you talked me into this."

We walk past a woman giving a blow job to a man while another man watched as he touched himself. This was one of Chicago's most exclusive adult parties, and it took me months to get an invite. The place was full of naked men and women openly exploring their sexual fantasies. Some people participated while others watched. Either way, it was erotic, and it was thrilling.

"It's not turning you on just a little?" I asked curiously.

The moaning sounds got my body hotter and my heart beating faster. I wanted to participate. However, I wasn't sure how far Casper would go. We were practically the most dressed ones there. Casper walked around in his boxers while I left my matching lace bra and panties on.

"What if someone here knows us?" Casper asked as he looked around. "Your brother will kill me. Literally."

"It's discreet. If anyone opens their mouth, they get banned. That's enough to keep everyone quiet."

"Since when have you gotten sexually adventurous?"

"Just want to try something new."

"You don't have to do that for me, Bethany," he said, kissing my cheek.

No, I didn't. It was more for me. My life was well ... imperfectly perfect. Depending on who you were—you either envied me or belittled me. Being the sister of the most powerful mobster to date—Luca DeCarlo, wasn't easy. My brother wasn't just a mobster; he was a Don. A Don is the highest status in organized crime—they are the boss of all bosses. We were like royalty in this city, but not in the way you'd think. Our name came with respect and fear—depending on who you were, determined which factored more into your obeyance. We were at the top of the chain, untouchable, and if you asked, it was no secret that my brother ran everything around here. Some girls would kill to be me but never know what that truly means. From the outside looking in, I had everything I could want, but from the inside looking out, I felt like a prisoner screaming to be set free. My life was laid out for me without much of my consent.

"How about we dip out of here and put on our own little show privately?" Casper smiled.

Smiling in return, I answer, "Fine."

Giving in was frustrating but nothing new. I've become so accustomed to doing what I was told I don't think I know how to make my own choices anymore. We began walking down a hall, and something caught my eye as we passed a room. Looking in as we walked by, I was stunned by the scene. It was like a stage with a large chaise sofa in the center. So much was happening that I couldn't fully process what I was seeing. A man was positioned on his knees fucking a woman who was lying on her back while a woman sat on her face, and another woman straddled her stomach, facing the man as he fingered her. Looking away as I continued to walk beside Casper, I couldn't help but be out of breath.

"Go ahead; I'm going to use the restroom," I bluffed.

"Okay, I'll meet you out front."

As Casper continued walking in the same direction, I slowly turned back toward the room. What was I doing? The closer I got to the room, the harder my heartbeat. Finding myself at the door, I stood watching and taking it all in. My eyes didn't know where to look first, but I was drawn into the heat of the moment. My eyes were fixated on the man, who not only kept this tempo at thrusting into the woman who lay on her back while fingering the woman straddling her, but his other hand grabbed the head of the woman who sat on the face of the first woman laying on her back and began aggressively kissing her. It was live porno in front of my eyes. The man's back had a large birthmark located behind his left shoulder that looked like a stain on his skin in the faint shape of a pear. Sweat glistened on his body, reflecting on the room's soft red lighting.

The woman getting fingered moaned in pleasure before noticing me in a trance watching them. She smiled and motioned with her finger to join. Startled by her noticing me, I began to panic. Suddenly, I felt ridiculous just watching them. Did I really think I'd participate? She whispered something into the man's ear before she climbed off the chaise and walked toward me. Part of me wanted to run, while the other was eager to stay. I was here for the experience, so why be a coward now? Wasn't the whole point of coming here to live outside the box I was cramped into?

"First time?" she asked as she approached me, noticing I wasn't completely naked.

Unable to respond, I nod my head. She was taller than I was by an inch; she had blonde hair just as I did. She walked behind me, standing close to my body.

"Just relax," she whispered into my ear.

Her fingers hooked around my panties, and she dragged them down as she lowered herself to her knees, removing them completely. My legs shook out of sheer panic. Turning around, I looked down at her as she smiled at me. I wasn't ready for this. Although I was curious, I just wasn't into women, and I was ready to bolt. Before I could step away, she placed her mouth at my opening. The feel of her tongue against my clit made my knees buckle as I tightly shut my eyes. Suddenly, I felt a hand grab my breast from someone standing behind me. My eyes shot open, and I saw a man's hand massaging my nipple over my lace bra while his other hand took my leg and draped it over the woman's shoulder, allowing her more access to move her tongue inside me.

A wave of electricity bolted through me as I breathed heavier. I refused to look over my shoulder or down at the woman, fearing I'd just run. I decided to live in the moment, for the first time, allowing myself to do what I wanted and no one dictating what I do. Allowing all of this to continue and let my body feel the surging orgasm, the sound of a tear made me look to the side to see the wrapper of a condom tossed on the floor. It quickly snapped me back to reality. I waited for someone to come in, ready to drag me out and be scolded, but nothing. This was really happening.

Wrapping his arm around my waist, I was lifted off my feet and placed on the chaise sofa on my hands and knees. It felt wrong to feel excited, and as badly as I wanted it, I was telling myself to get up and leave. But it didn't take long before the man was inside me, and I didn't stop it. The other women in the room stood there just watching. Were they judging me? Could they see on my face that I was tormented, whether this would be enjoyable? I shouldn't be doing this. My mind was spinning and going into overdrive. I wanted it so badly that I was willing to risk my good-girl reputation for a moment like this. As he continued to slide inside of me, I needed to make a choice before things really went too far. When I open my mouth, nothing comes out, and it's not because I can't speak; it's because I don't really want to stop this. Who knows when this could happen again, so I might as well go through with it and store this in my bank of memories.

Once fully inside, I let out a breath of relaxation. This man had girth and must have known it to start gently, but once my body felt it was in a comfortable position, he began thrusting inside me. Grabbing my ponytail with one hand and slapping my ass with the other, I wondered why none of my boyfriends ever did this with me. This was the spiciest thing I've had happen during sex. I never thought I'd enjoy something like that. He slanted his hips slightly, which hit a spot that made me gasp. As he continued to fuck me, it didn't take long before I was moaning nonstop and letting out a high-pitched orgasm. I think he hit my G-spot—also something that has never happened to me. I came as quickly as I could breathe but let the man wasn't done yet. After a few more thrusts, the man's body went rigid, and he let out a groan, which was a complete turn-on. That was another first. None of my boyfriends made a sound when they finished—some made a funny face or, like Casper, who just shut his eyes tight. I didn't know a simple reaction as a groan would make sex even better. I lay on my stomach, still catching my breath as my body was limp from the most intense orgasm from a stranger.

Then came another first. The man pulled away, sliding off the condom and tossing it on the floor before leaving the room. When I caught my breath, I turned onto my back, finding the room empty. The rush of excitement was gone and in flooded shame. Feeling used, I got up and quickly left the room. I wasn't that kind of girl. I was the girl who didn't have one-night stands. Although ashamed, I didn't regret what happened. That's what confused me the most. I rush toward the exit that leads to the cubbies that hold your belongings. Quickly, I got dressed, realizing I had never picked up my underwear. Too nervous to return to the party, I just left without it. On my way out the door, the man who greeted us at the party watched whoever was leaving.

"Hope you enjoyed yourself," he said, handing me a small square business card. "In case you are interested again."

Taking the card from him, I politely smile and find Casper waiting outside.

"What took so long?"

I took a deep breath, "Bathroom had a line."

Casper wrapped his arm around me, "Let's go to my place."

"I'm ready to call it a night," I replied nervously.

After what I just experienced, I couldn't sleep with Casper. It felt wrong. The tinged of guilt began to eat at me. I just cheated on my boyfriend. Casper wasn't even a thought in my mind or a reason to stop me from what I did. He wanted some action for himself tonight; I knew it. He may have played it off that the party didn't turn him on, but I knew that wasn't the case. But I didn't know how I would be able to enjoy anything with him after what I just did.

"I'm guessing we can put these parties on our bucket list as crossed out and done with?"

I nod my head, hiding my disappointment. "Totally."

As I lay in my bed, the night replayed in my mind. That was the most scandalous thing I've ever done, and for the first time, no one was around to reprimand me. It felt exhilarating. Just thinking about the man's touch had me tingling on the inside. Unable to fall asleep as images replayed in my mind, I reached toward my nightstand and pulled out my vibrator that was tucked away next to a bible my mother gifted to me.

Chapter 2

"Casper!" I giggled as he nibbled on my neck.

"I love the smell of you," he mumbled into my skin.

We were in the back seat of his car, and the windows were fogged up from our deep and rapid breathing as our mouths never parted while slowly undressing ourselves. After the sex party, my sexual appetite was like no other. I was dying for another explosive orgasm without having to attend a party to get it. So I did the next best thing: I tried to train Casper. At first, he was hesitant but eventually began to get into it. Parked in one of Chicago's secluded areas overlooking the city skyline, no one would interrupt what I had in store for tonight.

"Don't leave a mark," I slap his shoulder.

Casper ignored my plea, and I didn't do much else to stop him. Lost in our world, a sudden blaze of headlights lights up the inside of the car.

"I think we have company," Casper tried blocking the light with his hands.

"It's probably another couple." I hopped on top of him, and his hands made their way to my thighs as I comfortably straddled him while removing my shirt.

Still blinded by the light, Casper squints, "Why the hell are their brights on?"

"Maybe they want a show."

With a smirk, "I guess another one of your fantasies will be coming true."

Smiling at the opportunity, the thrill alone was enough to get me off. Quickly removing his shirt, our lips locked once again as I felt his hands trying to undo my bra. We've done this so many times you'd think he would have that part down by now, but he still seemed to struggle with it. Reaching behind me to remove it myself, our mouths never separated. As his erection grew through his pants, we both smiled through our kiss, knowing we would both leave satisfied. However, that quickly changed once we heard glass shattering around us. Startled by the sudden attack, I screamed while Casper froze in shock.

It happened so fast. The windshield's smooth glass was shattered into a million cracks. Before we could process what was going on, the driver and passenger windows were busted open. A hand reached into the driver's side and unlocked the doors. The backseat doors opened, and hands reached into the car from both sides—one pair pulling me out on one side while the other pulled Casper to the other. Terrified was an understatement; I was shaking uncontrollably. Once pulled out of the car, I was immediately covered with a jacket.

"Get off of me!" I shouted as I kicked and wailed my arms around.

I was tossed over the person's shoulders and carried to the other side of the car. Placed back on my feet, I make contact with a pair of dark and angry-looking eyes, instantly sending me into pure panic. I knew this was bad, and there was no getting out of this in peace.

This is how everyone felt when being around Chicago's leader: the man, the legend, the owner of this city—my brother, the one and only Luca DeCarlo.

Although my brother was always kind to me, in this moment, I never feared my brother the way I did now. He stood there unphased by one of his goons punching and kicking Casper.

"Please. Stop. Please." I was begging as I stepped forward.

"Make sure to break a rib," Luca says to the one kicking Casper as he looks at me.

"Don't hurt him," I plead at the sound of Casper whimpering in pain as he was kicked repeatedly in the ribs.

At the sound of a cracked rib, I took a step forward but was being held back by arms that wrapped around me, which only caused me to fight against it.

"B, calm down. It's me."

"Fuck off, Alfie!" I shout back, trying to get out of his grip.

Alfie was a 20-year-old that my brother took under his wing. We usually got along unless we got into moments like this where he obeyed my brother's command regardless of how I felt about it. Alfie handed me his jacket to fully cover myself as I watched Casper on the ground with a bloody face and bruised body. Falling to my knees beside him, I was again taken and held back. I knew better than to scream or shout—that would only make it worse for Casper.

My brother looked at me with disgust. "I've tried to be open-minded about who you date, Bethany, but it becomes a problem when I hear around town that my little sister is being used like a fucking whore."

"What are you talking about?"

"Don't play stupid."

"It's not what you think." I tried to sound calm, knowing that if I raised my voice or argued, he wouldn't listen to a word I said.

"How do you know what I'm thinking?" Luca spat out.

Beside Luca was his right-hand man, Emilio, who stood watching. Being in the room with either was scary enough, but you could feel your soul leave your body when you were in both their presence. I've heard what they were capable of. My brother had no limits, and Emilio was his right-hand man for a reason.

Emilio just smirked and then nodded to a bloody Casper on the floor. "What do you want me to do with the kid?"

I hated it when I was treated like this. Casper and I weren't kids. Luca stood over Casper with no pity. Someone of his status wouldn't be seen doing this or bother making an appearance when sending someone a message, but this was Chicago; my brother could be standing over a dead body holding the bloody knife, and no one would touch him.

Looking at me, Luca put the ball in my court, "B? What is a fitting punishment?"

Luca wasn't asking because he was being sympathetic. It was his way of allowing me to fix a wrong or make a choice he would approve of.

I bow my head in defeat. "I don't even know who he is. He's just a stranger to me."

Nodding his head, "Alfie, bring her to my car."

As I was escorted away, I could hear my brother telling Emilio to have someone drop Casper to the hospital. That was my reward for agreeing to cut ties with my boyfriend altogether. I didn't want to think about the alternative if I chose otherwise. Teary-eyed, I stood by the car in silence. As someone with everything at their feet, I often felt lonely.

"Come on, B," Alfie said as he handed me my clothes. "Luca won't hurt him. Just wants to scare him off."

I turn my back to him. Next to my brother's Bentley Continental was Emilio's Audi R8 V10 Decennium, and Alfie's Ducati Diavel 1260 was beside his. They came separately, which means this was a spontaneous visit and not planned.

"Whose big mouth spoiled it?" I demanded as I put on my bra and shirt.

"You know that's above my pay grade," Alfie replied.

I turn around to face him. "You're a good kid, Alfie. Why are you getting mixed up in this?"

Several times, I hit him with this question, but he must have been frustrated tonight.

He shot back with austerity, "I have no one, Bethany. I'm an orphan. Luca's treated me like family more than any foster parent has. It doesn't bother me if that means getting my hands dirty. You might not realize it, but your brother is a good man—he turned my life around. You don't have to see it the same way I do."

"I see more in you than you give yourself credit for."

"Alfie!" I hear Luca's voice call him over. Quickly, Alfie left me to attend to my brother.

As Alfie walked away, Emilio approached me with a cigarette in his mouth. His cigarettes were specially made. He didn't smell the part of someone who consistently smoked—instead, his scent was a mix of mint and eucalyptus. There was something about him that stirred an odd emotion within me. I wasn't sure if I was scared of him or intrigued. That's always been the case with him. He dressed well, as always, with a look in his eyes as though he was ready to set the city on fire at any moment.

Emilio has been with the family for as long as I can remember. I was ten years old when I first met him, and I remember he wasn't like everyone else. Growing up in a comfortable lifestyle surrounded by the same social status level of people, Emilio had an edge that was new to me. At first, it scared me but eventually I warmed up to him. He dressed ruggedly and spoke differently. My mother told me that's how people from the Southside of Chicago are. They were not bad people; they were just tougher and had more street smarts. Now, Emilio is dressed in the best suits, yet he still has never lost that edge. He was an asset to the DeCarlo Family, and even I knew his word held more weight than mine. The scar that cut through his left eyebrow intensified his demeanor. Emilio is one of those men you instantly know not to mess with.

"Why the long face, Bethany?" he asked. Emilio was the only person close to me who never called me by a nickname. It was always a formal Bethany.

"Is that a serious question?" I spat out.

"You shouldn't be surprised by this anymore." Emilio lit up the cigarette in his mouth.

"I'm tired of my brother interfering with every part of my life. It's not fair. I'm 25 and still treated like a child."

"Stop acting like one then," he let out a puff of smoke.

The smoke swirled around him in a captivating way. Or maybe it was just me losing my mind. Since the sex party, all I could think about was how that man made me feel, and now I was on a chase to get the same high. My body craved to be touched and satisfied.

"B, get in the car," Luca voiced as he reached the driver's side of his vehicle.

Emilio walked toward his car as another vehicle pulled up with two men who picked Casper off the ground. Alfie sped off on his Ducati without a goodbye. The last thing I wanted to do was get into the car with Luca, but I had no choice.

Luca sped off, and it was silent for the first two minutes.

"What were you doing there?"

I looked out the window as my arms were crossed against my chest. "Do I need to give you details?"

"You know what today is."

Suddenly, I became nauseous. I knew what day it was, but unlike the rest of my family, I wouldn't stay home and wallow in the past.

"It was 15 years ago," I replied.

Luca slammed on the brakes, causing me to jolt forward with the seatbelt digging into my skin. "Look at me," he demanded.

I turn my head to face him.

He was livid at my lack of empathy. "I don't care if it's 100 years ago. We may have lost Marco, but we won't forget him."

Marco was the eldest DeCarlo, who was gunned down in front of my parent's home along with his wife and child. It was hard for my family, but Luca suffered it the most. He was there when it all happened. He watched it all go down. That was the day that changed my family forever.

"He wouldn't want us moping over it."

"This day is like a black cloud that lingers over my head. And to get word that you are being a puttana on the anniversary your brother was killed is just disrespectful."

I huffed. There was no arguing over this. There was a time when Luca was happy and carefree. That all changed when Marco passed. Our family was in the lifestyle with our father being the Underboss to the late Don Vincenzo Baricelli, who at the time was the only mob family in Chicago who controlled everything.

Marco was well known and respected enough that people knew not to mess with his younger siblings, especially Luca and me. Our older sisters Rita and Isabella were closer in age to Marco, while Luca and I were younger. All Marco wanted for us was to find a path of our own. Unless you were directly a child of a Don, then no title was ever passed to you; it had to be earned. The title of Underboss was to fall onto Marco. He knew no other path for himself and knew there was no stability for us if we chose the same. Luca was set to play professional soccer overseas straight out of college, and I attended a prestigious private school. All was going accordingly until his death, which led Luca into the lifestyle, and it's what drove Luca to where he is now.

My brother didn't get to where he was easy; although I don't know the details, I did know he sacrificed a lot. But why did our name have to also fall onto my shoulders? I didn't choose this for myself.

"I went to the cemetery this morning and spent the day thinking about him," I defended myself. "Sorry that my boyfriend wanted to take me to dinner."

"Ex-boyfriend," Luca pointed out. "And I guess I'm too old to understand that dinner means getting a quick fuck in the back of a car."

"Well, a decade age difference has that effect."

Luca hated it when I got smart with him. "Bethany." He let out a breath of air. "Out of all days." His eyes never left the road. He wasn't an emotional man though I could sense his fragile state through his tough facade.

"I'm sorry."

Turning into my building, we again fell into silence. Luca took care of me; I never lacked anything. He bought me my condo, and I have access to his black card without him imposing a limit. I know I should be grateful, and I am; I just wish I had more freedom. I went to college out of state, but the tradeoff was to return home and hold my role as a member of this family. Little did I know what that truly meant. I may not have accepted his offer if I had known that my brother would dictate my life. But Luca would have found a way to get me in line somehow. Once he was crowned a Don, there was no going back to a normal life.

Luca parked his car in front of the complex and turned it off, but one of his hands remained on the steering wheel. I had a weird feeling in the pit of my stomach.

"Go in and pack a few things. You'll be staying with me for a little."

"Luca," I did my best not to get loud as I protested, "I give you my word, I won't see Casper again. There's no need to keep a direct eye on me."

"It's not about Casper," Luca turned to look at me. "I trust you, B, even if it doesn't always seem that way. I need you to trust me right now."

Trust was never an issue with my brother. "What's going on, Luca?"

"Some old friends from California are in town."

My stomach dropped. Old friends meant rivals or frenemies. Although California was a second home for Luca, it didn't always harbor good memories.

"Why are they in Chicago?"

"I sold the vineyard in California."

"You sold Sandra's vineyard? To who?" That was big. The vineyard held sentimental value to Luca, and he swore he'd never sell it unless something told him it was time to let go. I'd never thought that day would come.

"A random woman—not affiliated. All illegitimate ties were cut off. Not many people are happy about it."

"Jesus, Luca," I replied. "What the hell were you thinking?"

My brother was always strategic in his plans, and this seemed erratic.

"It's a power move."

"Is it supposed to backfire like this?"

"It was a considered possibility." Luca looked calm, and I wondered how he could do that under such circumstances. "Antonio will like having you around."

I smirk, "Of course, use my nephew against me."

"He'll need the company when I fly out."

"To where?" I question.

"Monthly meeting with the trio."

Luca referred to themselves as the trio, but they were known as *il Codice*. In Italian it means the Code. It was made up of the three most powerful Dons in the country. Any other families were below them. It was an entire hierarchy system put in place. It was like a democracy for made-men. The

DeCarlo Family, the Baricelli Family, and the Morrechi Family were the gods of mobster life. Every other family fell in line according to what the three would allow, and they always had some cut, which made sure money flowed into their pockets and anything else they had invested.

Luca waited in his car while I packed a few things. When I got back into the car, he was on the phone. I knew exactly who was on the other line by how he spoke. Sitting in the passenger side, I could faintly hear his response.

"Make sure to send a clear message. Anyone who wants to has an issue—to get over it or face the same fate."

"Will do," Emilio replied.

"Make sure to make it messy."

"My favorite."

My brother had no issue going to any lengths to get his way, and Emilio went to any length to ensure that would happen.

Chapter 3

I was walking into the kitchen, where a cook made breakfast and a housemaid laid everything on the table. Luca sat with his son; his demeanor was completely different. It was the only time you'd see my brother look at peace. When Antonio was born, Luca knew his fate was already set out for him. Being a son to a Don was a huge responsibility, and he had to be the successor to the family. Luca sacrificed his happiness to ensure the family was cared for and never had troubles. He wasn't just a Don to us; he was the patriarch of this family, and we all leaned on him. I watched Luca and Antonio interact as I made myself a cup of coffee.

"Your plans this weekend are to stay home," Luca told Antonio.

"Dad, come on! The soccer team is throwing a party; it will look bad if I don't go. They already hate on me being a freshman for making varsity."

"You're a freshman in high school; what are you doing at a senior party?"

Antonio didn't answer, and as his favorite aunt, I had to swoop in to defend him.

"You never listened to Mother when she told you to stay home," I smiled as I sat at the table with them.

Luca looked at me, "And that's why he will stay home."

In truth, the real reason was his fear of the outside visitors from California. Luca was set to fly out in a few days, and leaving Antonio behind, I knew, was hard for him to deal with.

"Can Stacey at least come over?" Antonio asked.

Luca shot him a look.

"And some other people," Antonio followed up with.

"Fine," Luca replied, "B calls the shots, though."

I gave Antonio a wink, and he got up from his seat, "Thanks, Dad. I'll see you when I get home. Brady is here—his mom is driving us to school. You want to come say hi?"

"No," Luca replied un enthused.

I couldn't help but laugh. Since Antonio was a little boy, all the moms at school would always try to speak to Luca as a chance to flirt with him once they knew he was a widower. They all fawned over him—the married ones the most. The less attention he paid to them, the harder they would try. Antonio ran off, leaving Luca and I at the table.

"Hopefully, you didn't have plans this weekend," Luca said.

"You know if I did, I'd cancel them."

"I asked Alfie to keep an eye on you while Emilio and I are away."

"It's unnecessary. I'll be here; it will be fine."

"He mentioned you've been pushing him to do something different with his life," Luca sipped his coffee.

Shifting in my seat, "I tell him that all the time."

"It's his choice, B."

"Well, you don't make it easy to turn away."

"I've offered to pay for schooling to become anything he wanted. He refused."

"It's a shame," I huffed.

"You did get him to voice what he did want."

"What's that?"

"More responsibilities."

Luca didn't need to go into specifics on what that meant. Alfie was set on this path by his own accord.

"He's just a kid. Not even old enough to drink."

"He turns 21 tomorrow. You and your friends should take him out."

Being closer in age to Alfie, I agreed. "Under one condition."

Luca already didn't seem thrilled. "It being reasonable."

"We take your Bugatti 16C Galibier."

CHAPTER 4

Club Chaos was on the south side and was always a hot spot in Chicago. Everyone from all over the city would go; it was the one place where it didn't matter what part of Chicago you were from. The place was blasting music you could hear whenever someone opened the door. Walking up to the bouncer with my two friends, Natasha and Tiffany, I smile and give him a wink. Times like this being a DeCarlo was worth it. Waiting in a line wrapped around the building wouldn't happen in 5-inch heels. We were let in, and the first stop was the bar.

"Hey Barbie, can I be your Ken?" a weak pickup line from a short man made me laugh. It wasn't the first time a guy referred to me as Barbie.

"How about you buy me and my friends a round of shots, then call it a night?" I replied as I bopped his nose.

He knew I was out of his league, but I gave him props for trying.

While attempting to get the bartender's attention, Tiffany shouted over the music, "Why aren't we at a table?"

"Because I don't want anyone to know I'm here," I shout back. "I just want to have fun before Alfie gets here without a thousand eyes on me."

"Umm, that's not possible," Natasha replied. "There's a reason why guys refer to you as Barbie."

I laugh at the reference and try to be modest, "I don't look like Barbie."

"You're right; Barbie has blue eyes and not green. What a shame."

Tiffany said, "If those long legs and blonde hair don't scream Barbie, then I don't know what does. Pair that with big tits, and you got yourself a Bethany DeCarlo."

"Ladies," Alfie appeared with a friend around his age. "This is Mark. Mark, this is Bethany, Natasha, and Tiffany."

I've never seen Alfie hang out with anyone besides the fellas, but it felt good to know he had a life outside the lifestyle. Maybe there's hope for him after all.

"How does it feel to drink legally now?" I shouted over the music.

"Not as fun," Alfie shouted back, "Something about doing things against the law is always more exciting."

"Boys will be boys," Natasha laughed.

"Our table is set up on the second floor," Alfie motioned for us to follow.

The club's second floor was open in the middle so that you can look down onto the dance floor. It was a bit quieter and more secluded.

"I've never seen you around," I said to Mark, who stood beside me at the railing, looking down onto the first floor.

"I go to college out of state," he replied. "I try to visit every once in a while."

"How do you know Alfie?"

"We met in one of the foster homes. We kept in touch. I'm graduating and have no job. Alfie said he would hook me up with something."

"What exactly is he able to hook you up with?" Alfie had no outside connections aside from my brother.

"Honestly, I don't care. My student loans aren't going to wait for me to get a good job to start paying them."

I nodded my head. "Well, good luck."

"Let's dance!" Natasha pulls me away and drags us onto the dance floor.

It wasn't long before men swarmed us. I was enjoying myself as I swayed to the music; a pair of hands grabbed my waist from behind me and pulled me toward their body as they grind against me. Looking over my shoulder, I saw it was an average-looking guy. Finding someone taller than you to dance with wasn't easy when I wore my high heels—I was already tall. To see the man fit my body to his perfectly made me flashback to the sex party, which shot a thrill through me. Grinding against him got more intense as the music played. I shut my eyes, picturing that night. His hands were on my hip, keeping me attached to his body. His head nuzzled against my ear as my head fell back onto his shoulder. One of his hands slowly moved down my thigh toward the hem of my dress. A crowd of people surrounded us. I wasn't sure who noticed, but at the same time, I didn't care. It felt good having someone touch me rather than use my vibrator. His hand went up my dress, creeping toward my core, but before his finger could even touch the surface, I felt his body completely ripped away from me.

It was instant and unexpected that I lost my balance and fell onto the floor. Annoyed, I look up and find Emilio glaring down at me. The man I was dancing with wasn't even in sight. He grabbed me by the arm and hoisted me to my feet without a word, dragging me off the dance floor. Taken to the back private room area, demanding the few people to leave, Emilio didn't let his grip go until we were alone and out of sight.

"What the fuck are you doing here, Bethany?"

"What does it look like?" I spat out, "Having fun. Like any other normal person."

"You're not just a normal person," Emilio replied, looking at me from head to toe. "You're dressed like a prostitute."

"It's the same thing every girl in here is wearing."

It was a black strapless mini dress with corset detailing on top and a sweetheart neckline. The bottom was a Milano rib jersey skirt that covered just enough. The underwired cups pushed my boobs up, making the dress look more provocative than it normally would on someone with a smaller chest.

"You're a DeCarlo. Your ass doesn't need to be shown to half of Chicago."

His words lit a fire under me. "Aren't you a bit old to even be here?"

Emilio smirked at my attempt to insult him. "Oh, you got me," he placed his hand over his heart, "My feelings are so hurt." He tried his best not to laugh.

"You work for my brother," I remind him, "You shouldn't be speaking to me this way."

"Flexing your muscle now, are you?" there was a gleam in his eyes as though he enjoyed the challenge.

His sarcasm got under my skin even more. He was known to be heartless, so nothing I could say would phase him.

"It's Alfie's birthday. I'm surprised you didn't know since you know every damn thing that happens." I had my hand on my hip and popped to the side.

"What I know is you were told to take him out. What I saw was you dry-humping some random guy on the dance floor."

"We were not–"

"His hand was up your dress in an open crowd of people."

Emilio wasn't wrong. It wasn't a good look at all. I had left the house feeling sexy and confident wearing this dress that looked a lot shorter on me, but it wasn't my fault I had long legs—especially with heels on.

"If you're going to tell my brother, just go ahead. Get it over with." I cross my arms against my chest.

"Is that how you think of me—a tattletale?"

"Right now, you don't want to know what I think of you."

The side of his mouth curved slightly in amusement, "I always love when people tell me about myself. You already called me old. What else ya got?"

I stared at him, thinking about a comeback. Emilio had to be in his mid-30s, not much older than Luca, and his wasn't phased by his age. Maybe I can pick on his outfit, but that wouldn't work either. He was dressed nicely in a black button-down and dark jeans. His gold chain that hung around his neck was visible as the top two buttons of his shirt were undone. In my 5-inch heels, we were eye to eye and I could slightly peek down his shirt.

The door swung open, and in walked a girl, "E, are you ready to go?"

Emilio turned his attention to her, "I'll meet you out front." Once she left, his focus returned to me. "How about this one time I cut you some slack? If you go home now, I won't say anything to your brother."

I place my hands on my hip, "You're bullshitting me."

"Maybe," Emilio shrugged, "But there are other things I'd rather be doing tonight than dealing with this."

Shifting on my feet in embarrassment, "So you are going to hold this against me instead?"

"Not if you go home."

"I don't want to go home," I protest.

"I'm not giving you an option."

"I'm not giving you an alternative."

Emilio clenched his jaw. "I'm not asking."

"I don't care."

"Okay."

I wasn't sure what to expect as he walked toward me, but I knew there was no way he'd lay a finger on me. But to my surprise, Emilio effortlessly threw me over his shoulder.

"What are you doing?!" I shouted as my perfectly waved style blonde hair was tossed around like a rag doll.

"Taking you home."

He carried me through the club to his grey-colored Maserati Gran Turismo parked out front and tossed me into the passenger seat. The smell of mint and eucalyptus was embedded into the black leather. Upset, embarrassed, and frustrated, I began to go off on him once he sat in the driver's seat.

"You can't do this!"

Unphased, Emilio replied, "I believe I just did." He sped off, driving as though he owned the road.

"This isn't fair."

"Saving you from embarrassment isn't fair?"

"Saving me?" I spat out. "You're the one who embarrassed me!"

"You should be thankful. Do you think no one knows who you are? I was approached five times by five different people about you being here. And I let it be. I never thought it would be true when I was told how you were behaving. If it were Luca there, how would it have gone down?"

Remaining silent about the information made me feel worse about myself. Emilio felt bad for me—I could tell. He should have interfered after the first person said something, but sometimes, he lets things slide as long as they don't get out of hand. Looking out the window, the tears streamed down my face. I felt something on my lap. Looking down, I saw Emilio handing me a handkerchief. It was the square pocket he always had paired with his suit of the day. The kind act made me even more embarrassed.

"A pretty girl like you shouldn't be crying," he said, trying to sound gentle.

"I don't need your pity," I sniffled.

"At least take this and wipe your face."

Taking the handkerchief from him, I wipe the tears that wet my skin. "Who carries these anymore?"

"I'm old, remember."

It made me laugh, but I still avoided eye contact and focused on looking out the window. We reach the house, and my stomach knots up. If Luca saw me walk in dressed like this, I wouldn't hear the end of it. Anything too tight, short, or see-through was not optional wardrobe attire. I was lucky to have left the house after he had gone out himself.

"He's not home," Emilio said, reading my mind.

"It's late. Where is he?"

"We all have needs, Bethany."

It took me a moment to understand what he was telling me. Luca was with a woman.

"His car...," I remembered, "I had driven it tonight and left it parked on the street."

"I'll take care of it."

Nodding my head, I get out of the car and go inside. The house was quiet as I walked through the foyer. The sound of my heels against the marble floor echoed through the house. Pulling my phone out of my bag, something fell out. When I pick it up, I realize it's the business card from the sex party. All it had was a phone number. I knew I shouldn't entertain it, but I couldn't help myself. An ache for thrill coursed through me, and I couldn't help but give in.

I dialed the number, and to my luck, there was a party tonight.

Chapter 5

The location was an abandoned warehouse, and the ambiance was completely different than the last time. On the outside, the building was run down and looked abandoned, but inside, it looked like a club. Stripper poles were placed throughout the floor, and the walls were all mirrors. The music was blasting and vibrating through the floor, sending chills up my body. Unlike the last party, where people stripped down before entering, clothing was removed along the way. Some people were naked, others half-dressed, and a handful, like me, were fully clothed.

I wasn't sure what to expect or whether I would participate, but being here made me feel alive. Slowly walking through the place, I figured getting a drink would help ease my nerves. I ordered a shot at the bar and down it quickly.

"Let me get gin straight," a man stood beside me ordering. "Can I get you a drink?" he asked me.

Interacting made me nervous, but there was no going back now. I was here, was there really any going back? Unsure if I could last here being sober, I smiled back and nodded my head to the man.

"I'll have a gin tonic," I tell the bartender.

"What's your name?" the man asks me.

Maybe I shouldn't give him a real name. "Brandy."

"Dillian," he extended his hand for me to shake. "First time here?"

"No," I replied as I returned his handshake.

He was also fully dressed in a plaid button-down shirt and khakis, which made me comfortable. He must have been new to this as well.

His smile lit up his face. "Want to take a walk around?"

"Sure."

It was a large space, and even though it was all open, there was so much going on you could barely tell it was one floor. As we people-watched, we had a conversation.

"What are you into?"

"Testing the waters."

Dillian nodded his head, "You're at the fun stage. Exploring a bit of everything."

We pass a woman dancing on a pole for a man who seems tentatively looking at her. She was topless and swung her body around like a professional. When I caught her face, she looked familiar. Where have I seen her? She let go of the pole as though it bored her and walked toward the man facing her. Ripping his shirt open, she peeled it off of him, exposing his back—it was the man with the birthmark on his left shoulder. Anticipation came over me; I needed to see his face. Gulping down my drink, I begin walking towards him. This was it. I can put a face to the body and hope that body would give me the same thrill as last time without the aftermath of the guilt.

"Where are you going?" Dillian asks.

"I'll be back," I said, unsure if that would be true.

As I walk toward the man, my legs completely give out. I hadn't realized how much I drank that night. Falling onto a couple seated on a sofa, fully naked and all over each other, they assumed I wanted to join. Their hands started exploring my body, something I wasn't ready for. Looking up to Dillian for help, he just watched without giving a helping hand. I shouldn't be panicking. After all, this was a sex party, but this felt all wrong. Feeling hands going up my arm, thigh, back, and chest, I struggled to get out of their grip, but suddenly, my body felt weak when their fingers tried to remove my underwear. Unable to push them away with enough force, there's a surge of arousal pulsing through me. The man and woman's touch started to feel sensational.

"Get the fuck off her."

The words rang in my ears. The man and woman were pulled off of me, and then I was tossed over a shoulder. The music playing pulsed through my body; I could feel it on my skin. As I was being carried away, I saw Dillian lying flat on the floor. If Dillian isn't the one carrying me, then who is? The odds of it being the man with the birthmark excited me, but looking down at the person's backside, I saw they were clothed, which was disappointing. I was taken outside, and the person yelled something out to one of the guards.

"You have bozos in there mixing shit into girls' drinks. Next time I catch this shit, the whole place is going up in smoke."

The man nodded. He looked scared, which made me giggle.

"Okay, you can put me down now," I said as I realized the man carrying me was walking away from the warehouse.

"You're going home."

A vehicle was parked around the warehouse in a secluded area, but I couldn't make it out. There was one light post, which was the only source of light. The night air was chilly but felt amazing against my skin. Finally placed on my feet, I looked up to see who this man was. My vision was blurry, and I couldn't stand properly alone. Leaning my back on the vehicle, I could only make out this man's dark features. Thick hair, high cheekbones, and black stubble covering his jawline gave him a mysterious look, but I was quickly distracted by his unbuttoned shirt that exposed his chest. His pants hung on his hip, exposing his v-cut, which gave me the urge to trace my tongue along it. Grabbing the loop of his pants, I pull him closer to me. Unexpecting the advancement, he falls toward me with both hands, landing on the top of the car, stopping him from making contact with me. As he came forward, the light from a lamppost exposed the man's face, and once I saw the scar cutting through his left eyebrow, I felt the blood drain out my face.

"Emilio?" I whimpered.

"What are you doing here?," he asked in a husky voice.

"What are you doing here?," I questioned in return.

My legs were shaky, and I didn't realize I was falling until he caught me.

"Didn't I drop you off? How did you get here?"

"It's barely midnight; why should I stay home?"

"You're fucking slurring your words, Bethany."

Was I? I thought I was speaking just fine. Emilio opens the door, forcing me into the passenger seat.

"What are you even doing here?"

Emilio looked annoyed, "Working."

I couldn't help but giggle, "Working? Like a sex worker?"

That seemed to piss him off, "Bethany," he breathed and remained as calm as he could. "Get in the car."

I would have pushed his buttons, but somehow, I felt drunker. Barely able to stand straight, I fell into the passenger seat. Emilio slams the door shut and swiftly walks to the driver's side. As I watch him walk around the car, his unbuttoned shirt is pushed back from a light brush of wind, exposing his torso. His obliques were perfectly sculpted. Did he work out? When did he have the time? When he was seated in the driver's seat, I blushed from my body reacting to checking him out. Emilio sped off without even glancing at me once.

The rush of watching the city fly past me as I looked out the window; the engine's humming vibration sent waves of static through my body, mixed with his scent, sparked strong arousal. It wasn't as though he smelt differently than before—for some reason, it was stronger tonight and doing something to me. When he said he was working tonight, what exactly was he doing? Was he a participant? The city looked different tonight. The color of the lights was bursting toward me, and I felt as though I could feel the outside air hitting my face as we drove.

I turned my head toward him and watched as he gripped the steering wheel with one hand and the clutch with his other as he switched gears.

"Did I ruin your night?" I asked.

Ignoring my question, "You shouldn't be at those parties."

"Why? Because people are having sex everywhere." rolling my eyes, "I know what sex is. I've done it before."

"That's not a place for someone like you to be."

"Ugh, here we go again with this."

"Luca finds out and will lock you in his cellar."

"Luca. Luca. Luca. All everyone cares about is what Luca will say, do, or think," I whined.

"Your brother built meaning behind the name DeCarlo. Something you clearly don't value."

"That's not true," I pouted, trying even to convince myself. Of course, I was proud to be a DeCarlo, but that didn't mean it made me happy. "You said you were there tonight working?"

"There's no need to go into details about it."

"You sound scared," I teased.

"Scared?" Emilio shot me a look, "Scared of what?"

"That Luca would find out how you spend your free time."

"Your brother doesn't need to know what I do in my spare time." Emilio looked at me with a concerned face and asked, "Are you feeling okay?"

"I only had a couple of sips, but everything is... a lot."

Emilio inhaled sharply, "Something was put in your drink."

"How do you know that?"

"Once I saw you, I knew something was up. That's not like you."

Right, of course not. "It's getting really hot. Can you turn on the AC?"

He blasts the air, and the coldness on my skin makes me pant. My body woke up as though life was sprung back into me, and I was loving it.

"Feels good?" The side of his mouth curved into a smirk as though he had a secret but said nothing.

I nod my head, "Mmhhmm."

"That prick from the party put something in your drink. Probably X. So you'll feel everything a bit more intensely."

"X? Like ecstasy?" I laugh, "We call it Molly these days, old man."

"There are a few names for it, sweetheart. Is it your first time on it?"

I nod my head. My hands touched my thighs; the bare skin-to-skin felt nice. I tilt my head back and close my eyes. Emilio was right—everything was intensified. All my senses felt heightened, and it was exhilarating.

"What are you doing?" Emilio asked.

Rather than reply, I let out a moan.

"Bethany. What the fuck."

Without realizing it, I had opened my legs and slid my hand in between my thighs to finger myself. I got lost in giving myself an orgasm. The sound of my fingers entering and exiting my soaked core was the only thing you could hear within the car aside from my moaning. Opening my eyes, I look at Emilio. It wasn't until he turned his head and we made eye contact that I saw he was affected. This only made me keep going.

He reached out his hand and grabbed my wrist to remove my hand from touching myself, but he was too late. I came, letting out a light scream. My body relaxed as I sunk further into the seat. I smirk from the satisfaction. But what was even more satisfying was seeing a look in his eyes. Me, Bethany DeCarlo, had Emilio out of character. He was in control of himself but gave a different type of energy. His grip on the steering wheel made his knuckles turn white. The hand on my wrist was giving off heat. I wanted more. Squeezing my legs shut in an attempt to keep his hand in place, I lean forward and place my hand on his bare chest, making my way down to his crotch, but his hand broke free.

Grabbing my wrist, Emilio sounded irritated, "I don't know what the fuck you are pulling here, Bethany, but cut the shit."

"Why?" I teased. "I don't turn you on?"

We pull into the driveway of Luca's home, and Emilio slams on the brake once we pass the gate. Still needing to go up the driveway, Emilio parked the car and got out. I watch him walk to the passenger side and open the door. Emilio pulled me out of the car, and I stood leaning against it as Emilio came face to face with me.

"This is the drug talking. You need to get your shit together before you go inside. You hear me?"

I wrap my arm around his neck while my other hand rests on his oblique. "Am I not your type?"

"Sweetheart, I'm all for a blonde with big tits, but you're messing with the wrong guy."

Boldy, I wrap my leg around him, pushing the limit. "Scared you'll get in trouble?"

After removing my leg from his hip, Emilio points his thumb behind him. "That camera behind me is pointing right at us. Your brother will see it once security flags something as an issue."

As I looked over his shoulder, on the fence, there was a camera pointed directly at us. Even though it was dark out, I was sure it had night vision. This place was scattered with security.

"The fearless Emilio is scared."

"I'm not the one who would be scared." Taking my hand, he places it in his pants over his boxers. He was rock hard. "I'll fuck you right here."

In shock by his bold move, I stood speechless for a moment. "You're bluffing."

Emilio closed the gap between us, taking me by surprise as I placed both hands up against his bare chest. He slowly began pulling up the hem of my dress, which was already short, so there wasn't much there. Pressing his erection into me, I felt my heart beating out of my chest. His face was getting closer to mine, and as our lips were about to touch, a bright light was cast upon us.

The light was blinding, and that's when I realized we would be seen on camera, and the fear of my brother finding out all came crashing down on me. Instantly, I push Emilio away. He looked at me as I adjusted my dress.

"That's what I thought."

Chapter 6

What just happened? The fear and shock sobered me up. Emilio had made me get back into the car to bring me to the front door. It was the longest few seconds of my life, and the silence was deadly. I could hear my heart pumping blood through my veins. I couldn't even look him in the face, and without a goodbye, I jumped out of the car, quickly reaching the front door. Shaking as I tried to get the key in, I didn't even check if Luca's car was parked outside. Too scared to look behind me, Emilio was still there. I could hear the engine of his car running. Once securely inside, I hear him speed off. The house was quiet, and the foyer light guided me to the staircase, where I removed my heels so I wouldn't wake anyone up.

"Ms. DeCarlo."

I jump, startled by the voice. Looking over my shoulder, I see it's the butler—I could never remember his name. "Jesus. You scared me."

"Apologies, Ms. DeCarlo. Would you like me to get you anything before you head upstairs?"

"No," I replied then continued up the stairs.

I quickly entered my room and tossed my shoes onto the floor. The sheer fright of what occurred had me on edge. My body was tingling on the line between feeling panic and being embarrassed. Entering the master bathroom attached to the room, I turn on the shower and remove my makeup and dress. Steam from the water fills the bathroom; the mirror begins to fog. Staring at myself, I barely recognize the emerald eyes looking back at me. Throughout the years, I slowly lost myself. Sex parties, drugs, throwing myself onto guys? That wasn't me.

Stepping inside the shower, I let the hot water soak up my skin. Nothing beats a hot shower. Instantly, I relax. When done, I grab a towel around my body and another around my wet hair. Walking back into the bedroom, I didn't even bother throwing on clothes. I want to lie in bed, fall fast asleep, and forget this night ever happened. Still wrapped in the towel, I rested my head on the pillow, and my eyes began to close, but all that relaxation faded once images of Emilio began popping into my head. My eyes shoot open. No. This can't happen. Shaking it off, I close my eyes again. All I could see was Emilio with his unbuttoned shirt, and recalling the smell of mint and eucalyptus had my insides stirring.

No. No. No. No. Opening my eyes, I turn on my side. I've never looked at Emilio in that way. But the look on his face and the tone of his voice when we stood by his car outside the gate just moments ago was etched into my brain. Replaying it, I felt as though I was reliving the moment. I could hear his voice which sent vibrations through my body; the feel of his erect cock pulsed against my hand, and before I knew it, my finger was inside me. This was wrong on many levels, yet there was this thrill. I knew Emilio would never cross that line in real life, but in my mind, we can do whatever we want. Maybe giving into my imagination will get me to fall asleep.

So I gave in. Picturing him as he stood before me with his shirt open, I began imagining how I would have done things differently. Instead of pushing him away, I would have pulled him in closer. At the thought of it, I entered another finger inside me. The more I imagined things going differently, the wetter I got as I picked up the pace of my fingers moving in and out of me. I was kissing him as he wrapped his arms around me while I tried pulling down his pants. My small moans filled the quiet room as I gave myself over to the sensations taking over my body. The orgasm was building, and I hadn't even gotten that far in my imagination, but I was enjoying myself. Picturing the feel of his cock against my core almost sent me over the edge. My body was about to go into overload as I was getting ready to orgasm.

Right as I was about to burst, there was a knock at my door.

"B, open the door."

The sound of my brother's voice immediately put everything to a halt. Quickly pulling my fingers out of me, I sat up as though I was caught in the act. Except I was in the room alone; Luca hadn't even seen me.

I gulped and took a deep breath before answering. "Everything okay?"

"I need to speak to you."

Shit. Luca's tone was serious. Not fully recovered from the effects of the alcohol; the walls felt as though they were closing in on me.

"Just got out of the shower; let me throw on something," I shouted as I scrambled to find a shirt and shorts.

Would Emilio have told him about tonight? If he did, I'd never see the light of day again. Once put together, I slowly approach the door, stalling on what lay on the other side.

Opening the door, I make sure to have a happy face on.

"Hey."

Luca makes his way into the room. I couldn't stop him if I wanted to.

"How was tonight?" He looks annoyed.

The question made my ears drum. Stay strong, B. "Good. How was yours?"

"Good. Although I walk in to hear that you came stumbling in a few minutes ago."

"I had a few drinks, totally sober now."

"Emilio said he dropped you off."

Shit. Shit. Shit. Shit. My brother was good at getting the truth out of someone by making them think he already knew. Was he doing the same thing now? I don't know. He was a good bluffer, so I stayed silent.

Luca went on, "Respect is a two-way street, Bethany. I understand you grew up in a more privileged environment compared to the rest of our siblings, but that doesn't give you the entitlement of looking down on people."

Huh? What the hell was he talking about? "Okay," was all I could think to say.

"Albert doesn't end his day until he is dismissed."

Who the fuck is Albert? "Right..."

"I told you after dinner to dismiss him when you get home. So why did I have to do it? It's 2 am. He gets up at 5 am, before everyone, to ensure the morning is properly set up for the entire house."

It hit me that he was talking about the butler. Albert was his name. "That's what you came to tell me?"

"Emilio just called me."

Vomit shot up my throat for a split second and I tried not to gag. I thought I dodged the bullet. "And?"

"I'm leaving to go to New York in the morning. I won't see Antonio off to school."

I sigh in relief, "I'll handle it, don't worry."

I didn't mind caring for Antonio while my brother was away, but he never did last-minute trips. Something had to be wrong.

"Is there an emergency?"

Luca looked at me blankly, "One of the New York families wants to speak to me personally."

I roll my eyes, "Since when have you taken the time of day to speak to someone below you at such short notice?"

"Someone mentioned something to Emilio that raised a concern. I need to know what that is."

"Emilio usually takes care of those things without you." Speaking Emilio's name was making me jittery.

"It's something I need to see with my own eyes. We won't be gone for long."

"I have you covered," I assured him.

Luca nodded his head and walked out. Shutting the door, I lean against it and sigh in relief. Emilio hadn't said a word. Thank god. As I approach my bed, my phone on the nightstand goes off. It was a text from Alfie.

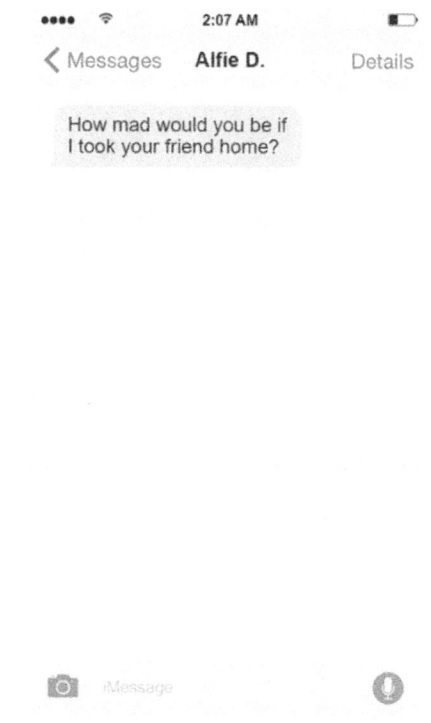

> **Alfie D.**
>
> How mad would you be if I took your friend home?

Rolling my eyes, I wasn't even going to answer. Placing my phone back on the stand, I hop on the bed. As I lay down, I got another message. Reaching for the phone, it was again Alfie.

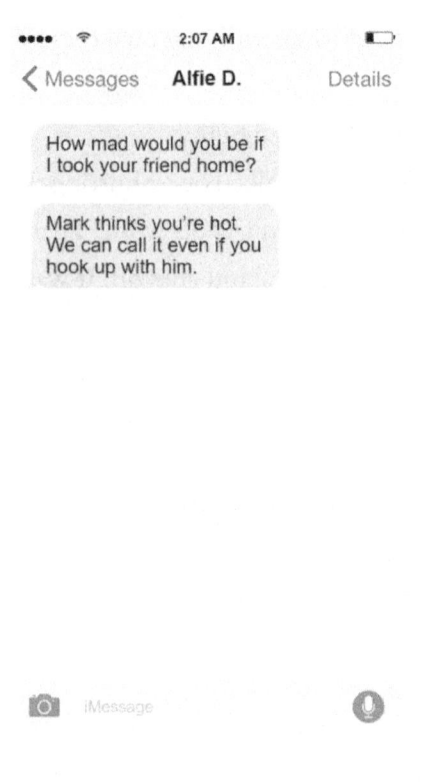

> **Alfie D.** — 2:07 AM
>
> How mad would you be if I took your friend home?
>
> Mark thinks you're hot. We can call it even if you hook up with him.

Ignoring the message, I place the phone on the pillow beside me, only for it to go off again. This time it was Natasha.

CONDEMNED

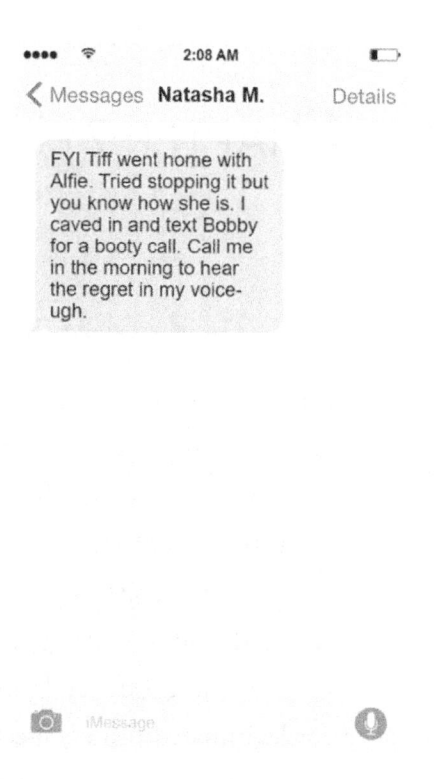

> FYI Tiff went home with Alfie. Tried stopping it but you know how she is. I caved in and text Bobby for a booty call. Call me in the morning to hear the regret in my voice- ugh.

Ugh. I toss my phone on the other end of the bed. Am I the only one not getting laid tonight?

Chapter 7

It's been three days with Emilio gone, which I thought would have allowed me to get bored of replaying different scenarios in my mind with him. But no. All I could think about was Emilio, which was frustrating. How many times can you masturbate to the thought of the same man?

Pulling up to my job, I look up at the sign. DeCarlo Sites. It was my brother's company, which I was the officer manager. Although working wasn't a necessity, it helped pass the time. Luca and Emilio weren't always in the office; it was saved for legitimate business meetings. They would conduct everything else at the lounge, where you'd mostly find them. After a boring day, I leave the office to pick Antonio up from school.

"Hey, B," Antonio popped his head into the car. "Can we take Stacey home?"

I smile, "Sure."

Boys always had it easier. Antonio having a girlfriend before he was even a teenager was completely fine; when I was his age, if a boy even tried to speak to me, he would get threatened. Antonio opens the back door to let his girlfriend in first, then slides in beside her. Watching them hold hands was cute, but then I wondered if they were doing other things.

"So, how is school?" I asked them.

"AP classes suck," Antonio replied. "How am I supposed to keep up with soccer practice at school and the travel team while keeping a good average?"

"I'm sure you'll manage."

"Ant is on varsity," Stacey smiled. "He should just step down from AP classes if soccer is his main focus."

I was impressed with my nephew, although not surprised; Antonio was good at soccer, maybe even better than Luca was at his age. "Your father will be proud. Not sure he'd make you drop AP classes."

Looking in the rearview mirror, Stacey rolled her eyes. She was stuck, but I tried to be nice for Antonio's sake.

"I know," Antonio replied, "But maybe if my favorite aunt would talk to him?"

I laugh, "Now I'm your favorite? You didn't say that when Rita bought you those limited edition sneakers."

Antonio smirked; he looked like Luca, with sandy brown hair and green eyes. "You know the others get jealous if I say it out loud. Plus, you and I both know your dad's favorite sister." He was a smooth talker, just like his father, knowing exactly what to say and how to say it.

"I'll see what I can do."

Antonio and Stacey carried on their conversation in the backseat.

"OMG," Stacey gushed, "Brit is having people over this weekend. Wanna go?"

"Michela has a dance competition. I told her I'd go."

I couldn't help but listen to their little quarrel. Antonio and Michela grew up together like siblings. It was clear Stacey viewed her as a threat even though Michela was older than they were and had no interest in Antonio in that way and vice versa.

"Seriously?" Stacey huffed.

"We can go after."

Antonio was like his father—he didn't like being told what to do and was unapologetic about his decisions. After we dropped Stacey home, we headed to my mother's for dinner. Antonio joined his cousins while I sat in the kitchen with my sisters as my mother cooked. It was like old times, before Rita and Isabella were married when Marco was alive, and Luca was the family's angel. I remember when Luca came home to tell us he was drafted to play soccer in Europe. Mother cooked his favorite dish as she always did for each child to celebrate their accomplishment.

"You know, when I was your age, I was married with my first kid," Rita told me. "When are you going to start your own family?"

"If your brother Luca can stop scaring off men!" I reply.

"Luca was nothing compared to Marco," Isabella chimed in. "Remember, he would third wheel every date!"

"Okay, maybe you guys had it worse," I laugh.

"Bethany, why don't you let Luca set you up with someone? He has so many connections," my mother smiled warmly.

"I don't know if getting married is for me."

The three of them looked at me as though I had ten heads. "What?!" they all said at once.

I shrug my shoulder, "What's so bad about that?"

"You're beautiful and smart," Rita said, "Wouldn't you want to pass those on to your future children?"

Isabella spewed with jealously, "Beth and Luca were the lucky ones getting those green eyes."

I stuck my tongue out at her. She was always envious of that.

"All my children are beautiful," my mother cut in. "But Rita is right; you should settle down."

"How about this? I'll marry when Luca does!"

The three of them shook their heads.

"So never," Isabella replies. "You know after Claire he swore off marriage."

Thinking of his deceased spouse, Claire, made me angry. She was selfish, always wanting more out of Luca than he could offer. She despised him for not loving her the same way she loved him, so she went on a suicide mission. Everyone plays it off as though she passed from an illness like cancer. But she had more of a mental illness. Luca found her locked in a car with their two children as the engine was on in the closed garage. Antonio was the only one who made it out alive. Claire and their daughter, Lilianna, who was only a month old, didn't survive.

"You would too if you were married to Claire," Rita blurts out.

"Rita!" my mother shouted.

"It's true."

"He wouldn't have married her if it wasn't arranged," Isabella added. "Too bad about Sandra."

This made the room go silent. No one mentions the name Sandra, especially around Luca. She was his first love and only love. He found her body floating in one of Chicago's fountains. When it came to love, Luca didn't have much luck.

"Mood kill," I said to Isabella.

"I still have hope for him," Rita voiced, "And I have hope for you too, Bethany."

Chapter 8

After settling in, I check on my brother. All the walls in the office were glass, so no one could ever hide from doing anything. I used to think it was part of the office's aesthetic, but I'm sure it's a security thing. As I approached his office, which was the only secluded one located away from everyone else, I saw Emilio standing there with one hand in his pocket as he spoke to Luca. This would be the first time I saw him since throwing myself at him. A reminder of the embarrassment was making me sick to my stomach.

My brother sees me approaching and nods to Emilio to open my door. As Emilio turned around, I felt my cheeks get red, and I began to get goosebumps while he looked as calm as ever. I didn't mind not seeing him since the shame of my actions stained me. Now face to face, I felt like I was wearing the scarlet letter.

"Bethany," he smiled and winked at me as he opened the glass door.

He has always greeted me by saying my name but never winked. Emilio barely ever paid me attention. Walking past him, I avoid looking in his direction. I approach my brother, seated on a chair beside a sofa. Like all the offices here, the middle of his office had a conversation area with sofas and a coffee table in the center.

"Sit B," Luca said.

As I did so, I could feel Emilio's eyes on me even though he was behind me. It was completely distracting.

"How was New York?" I asked.

"Fire the developer I have for the project out in the Land Ends."

Confused, "What? Why?"

Luca was creating an area within Chicago that was like its own city. It was expected to generate 90% of the city's revenue. It was strategically placed in the first part of Chicago my brother owned when it was a dump. No one wanted to be in that area back then, but now it's one of the city's wealthiest areas.

"I'm signing on someone new," Luca replied.

"Who? You already had the best developer on it."

"Aria Cassariano."

The name Cassariano caused my brain to malfunction for a moment. "You hired a Cassariano?"

"Soak it in, get upset, and then get over it." Luca didn't even seem phased.

"Get over it?!" I couldn't help but raise my voice as I got to my feet. "They are responsible for Marco's death, and you want me to get over it?!"

The name Cassariano was not welcomed in Chicago for several reasons. One is that they were responsible for Marco's death. I never understood why Luca didn't obliterate that entire family. Lorenzo Cassariano was the king of New York but didn't stand a chance going against my brother. The Cassarianos have ties to the Baricelli Family, which was a sticky situation. Domenico Baricelli was head of the Family, succeeding his father, Vincenzo. Domenico gave the city of Chicago to Luca as a thank-you gift—as to what he was being thanked for, only select people knew, and two of them were in this room with me. Luca was loyal to Domenico, so when he was asked to put the whole ordeal behind him, he did.

"It's an opportunity to get some insight on what's going on in New York and what they have up their sleeve."

"Are you fucking kidding me, Luca?!" I reply, speaking through my teeth. "Just a few weeks ago, you freaked out on me for going out with my boyfriend on the anniversary of Marco's death, but you... you want a Cassariano in this city working under your roof, and I'm just supposed to be okay with it??"

"Once I know what they are up to, Aria will be out of here. But for now, we play nice."

"Wait til Mother, Rita, and Isabella hear about this," I pout.

"They will only hear about it if you tell them."

"You don't think they will find out on their own?" I was annoyed.

"Let them. By the time they do, I'm sure she'll be gone."

I was pretty sure Luca was lying, but who am I to argue with his plan? "Fine."

"You'll make sure she settles into the office. Try and get to know her. Be friends."

"Right," I shake my head in disbelief. "Is there a crash course on how to friend a rival into being your bestie?"

"This is a curveball for everyone," Luca replied. "Just do your best. Tell Emilio immediately if anything sounds odd or there's odd behavior."

In the heat of the discussion, I forgot Emilio was in the room. Now, I stiffen at the sound of his name. I can barely make eye contact when he walks into sight and I feel like I'm on fire.

"Are you okay, B?"

"Yes, I'm fine," I reply to Luca.

"You're beet red."

"Am I?"

"Why don't you go lay down for a second? Emilio, make sure to make that call we talked about." Luca was dismissing us.

"Will do," Emilio replied.

As we headed toward the door, I stopped short to avoid colliding with Emilio, who reached for the door to open it. I just wanted to get out of here, but Emilio walked beside me as I made my way to my office.

"You didn't tell Luca?" I asked, avoiding contact as I looked straight ahead.

"Of course not. You'd be locked in the basement til someone found your corpse."

I tried to laugh, but the truth wasn't funny. "Did you need something from me?"

"Wanted to check on you. Make sure you're okay."

"On me?" I question. "Usually, that's Alfie's job."

"Last time we saw each other, I was close to fucking your brains out on my car. Just want to make sure there were no mixed or conflicting thoughts."

I was stunned that he said it as loudly as he did in an open area. "What conflicting thoughts could I possibly have?" My body temperate rose to the point of making me actually sweat.

Sensing I was uncomfortable, Emilio chuckled, "Relax."

I blurt out, "I am relaxed."

"I can tell."

A tight smile crosses my face, "What happened was inappropriate. I was out of line."

"I agree. I would have liked to be taken out to dinner first. I'm not that kind of man, you know."

Not wanting to appear as though I couldn't handle a joke, I had to play something back. "You strike me as someone who puts out on a first date. Figured I'd skip the dinner part."

"No hard feelings?"

"No," I reply.

"Good." A smirk crossed his face. He winked and went on his way.

I inhale the last bit of his scent before he walks off. Hard feelings? It's more like sexual desires. I wish I had the guts to cross that line with Emilio without remorse, but I knew that wasn't possible. Not having him, I was hoping wouldn't become an obsession. To think I'd be able to get Emilio Pugliese was laughable. What could Emilio, the infamous Consigliere of Chicago's mob boss, possible have to offer anyway? The imaginative thoughts I had of him became so vivid in my mind. It shook me to the core.

Chapter 9

My distraction was getting our staff ready for Aria's arrival. It was a big deal for a few reasons. Not everyone on staff in the office was entangled in my brother's illegitimate affairs, but there were enough to know this project was big, and it took a lot of pulled strings to get approvals and permits. Some were on edge about having Aria around, and I was curious to meet the woman who finally had everyone by the balls.

She was set to arrive today but would start working on Monday. Luca had her stay at his hotel, the Lagos. The hotel had a penthouse that was Luca's second home, usually where he would take women for the night. My brother never let a woman into his home other than his family. I wasn't expecting Aria to be placed in the penthouse, but it made sense since it was heavily surveilled.

On my way out, Luca calls me.

"Have plans tonight?"

"If I did, I'm sure you are calling to tell me to cancel them."

"Good. We are going out tonight."

"We?" I asked. "As in you and I?"

"Alfie mentioned you were having a rough week."

Rough didn't cut it. Setting up for Aria's arrival was a nightmare; everyone had questions about every detail.

"Your treat," I reply.

"Isn't it always."

I wasn't exactly sure how to dress. Still, seeing that Luca was wearing dark jeans and a leather jacket, I opted for the same—picking out my tightest skinny jeans and a matching black color tube top paired with a cream leather jacket and red bottom heels topped off with a matching clutch. I was ready for whatever Luca had in store. Driving his all-black Bugatti La Voiture Noire, he flies down the streets of Chicago. Even on the roads, people seemed to clear the path for him.

"Can you tell me now where we are going?"

"Club Chaos."

I was surprised at his response. "For?"

"Aria should be there. Would be nice to meet out in a social setting."

"I thought this was all business, no play with the Cassariano girl."

Luca smiled, "Sometimes you just have to jump in a mud puddle because it's there."

"That sounds... messy."

As we pull up to the alley behind the club, we see a group of people outside. They were all squinting from the headlights pointed at them. I saw Emilio there with other men who surrounded a man I had never seen before. A woman stood to the side watching them. Seeing Emilio in his navy suit looking so good made me nervous to the point that I was ready to jump out of the car and run home.

"Shit." Luca spat out.

He jumped out of the car, and I could hear the conversation.

"What's going on here?" Luca demanded.

"They were just leaving," Emilio replied as he turned to Luca.

Luca then looked at the woman. I had no idea what was happening, so I jumped out of the car and approached my brother.

"I'll be inside," I said to Luca, touching his arm.

But he focused solely on the woman, and I could see why. She was beautiful. She had long black hair, olive skin tone, light brown eyes, and the perfect body with her small waist and curvy hips. I left them outside and entered the club through the back to wait in the private room. A few minutes later, Luca and Emilio came inside.

"You think they are together?" Luca asked.

"Doubtful," Emilio replied, "But that shouldn't be your concern. There's a bigger issue."

My brother did not look happy. "If you're going to ruin my night even more, I don't want to hear it. Figure it out."

Emilio cleared his throat, "The Appollo brothers are here."

In irritation, Luca took a deep breath, "Get them out."

"They want to talk to you. Gabe claims they know something you don't want to be made public."

"Bullshit," Luca replied.

"That's what I thought, but the fact they flew into Chicago without a worry has me thinking it must be serious. The Appollo brothers don't have those kinds of balls to bluff."

"Nothing that could be of concern to me."

Emilio leaned in and whispered something to Luca, which seemed to have gotten his full attention.

"Where is Alfie?"

"He's out there with the redhead."

When Luca looked confused, I said, "Aria's assistant, Molly."

His confusion turned to annoyance, "Take the brothers to the back showroom.

The showroom was another room at the club that held private parties. The kind of private parties hosted to cater to men's guilty pleasures all for the sake of doing good business. After Luca searched for Alfie, Emilio motioned for one of the men to carry out the order.

Emilio and I were left together. Unsure how to act, I stood there looking anywhere but in his direction.

"Nervous?" Emilio asked.

Stunned, I reply, "No."

"You haven't stopped tapping your foot."

I smile and divert the conversation. "So, who was Luca talking about?"

"Aria and Gio. Your brother seems to think they are sleeping together." Emilio found it amusing.

"Why does it matter?"

"You're too young to remember or even know. Gio was a captain under Baricelli for the Southside a long time ago. He faked his death and became Consigliere to Aria's brother."

"How did he manage that?" I replied, shocked.

You don't leave a family unless it's by death, and death only.

"Long story."

"And no one has tried to... you know."

"Another long story. Plus, Consiglieres are off limits. No one touches them. Unless the boss himself offs him. Or in this case, Cassie." Emilio laughs.

"Cassie? Your sister? Why would she?"

"That's her husband."

Shocked, I replied, "I didn't know she was married."

"His name doesn't get spoken about around here. I can't believe the idiot set foot in this city." Emilio took a deep breath, "He was lucky to have Aria with him tonight."

"You said Consiglieres are off limits."

"I wouldn't go to him as a Consigliere, I'd go to him as a pissed off brother. He broke Cassie's heart."

"E," one of the guards walked in. "Everyone is in place."

"Thanks," Emilio nodded.

As he walked away, he spoke over his shoulder in my direction. "You should stick around. Get to know that redhead who works for Aria. She will be a good source."

Just like that, on cue, Alfie came in with a stumbling Molly.

"Hey, B. You mind?" he asked me while plopping the redhead onto the sofa.

"Seriously, Alfie? I didn't come out to babysit."

Alfie walks up to me, "Luca just ripped me a new one, having Molly here, especially for tonight. Just watch her for a bit, please?"

"What do I get out of it?" I question. "And it better be fucking good."

Leaning in, almost whispering, "I'll let you know what happens at the meeting."

"What makes you think I'd care about that?" I bluffed.

"Inside information isn't always a bad thing."

"Isn't that against what you're supposed to do? Luca would be disappointed."

"As long as he doesn't know. Plus, it's for you. You're family."

I roll my eyes. "Fine. But I want all the details."

Alfie winked at me. "Thanks, B!"

As I turned to face Molly on the sofa, she sat there happy. She's drunk. Great.

"Hey," I say as I sit beside her. "Having fun tonight?"

"This place is nothing like the clubs in California," she hiccupped.

"Is that a good or bad thing?"

"Good, I guess. Chicago in general—it's different. You're the office manager, right?"

"I am," I reply, sounding as if I was so proud of it. Being nice to these California people is already annoying me.

"You're like, really pretty."

I smile, "Thank you."

For however long, Molly and I sat chatting. Thankfully, she was drunk and didn't notice my asking about Aria. I learned a few things, and I was impressed. Molly didn't know all the details, but piecing what she did say, the rumors were true. She broke away from her family. She chose to walk away and only reunited years later when her father passed. Part of me didn't know how to feel about that. How can someone walk away from family? Even when there were those times I despised being a DeCarlo, never did it cross my mind to leave.

Would I ever muster the strength to walk away?

After an hour, Alfie walks back in, but alone. I stood up to meet him so that Molly wouldn't hear anything Alfie had to tell me.

"Good news or bad news first?"

"I don't like the fact there is bad news," I replied.

"Well, there is. So, which one first?"

I huff, "Make me smile, then break my heart."

"You'll get to live in California like you always wanted."

"What?" I spat out in surprise. California was made for me. It broke my hear when I had to leave after college.

"Don't get too hyped; that's only happening because Luca offered your hand in marriage to Gabe Appollo."

"What?" I spat out again in surprise.

Chapter 10

"What?" I spat out again in surprise.

Alfie shrugged, "I didn't get much of the conversation; your brother was the only one speaking to them—Emilio wasn't even allowed. I overheard Luca telling Emilio afterward. He made it sound like it needed to happen ASAP."

Rage filled me from the inside out. "I refuse for that to happen."

Alfie looked at me with pity, "I'm sorry."

I watched him walk off toward Molly as I stood in place. The same anger I continuously push down started to build up again. What was wrong with my brother? How could he use me like I meant nothing to him? This couldn't be the life I was told to have. It's not fair. After hearing Molly talk about Aria gave me hope that I, too, can break free from the lifestyle I am held captive in. The first thing I'd need to do is get out of this, and any other arranged marriage my brother has planned for me.

"Alfie," his name came out my mouth as a demand, "Where is Luca?"

"Probably still in the showroom," Alfie replied as Molly sobered up and hung off him.

I started walking away without another word, but Alfie knew without me having to say where I was going.

"B! Don't."

But I was no longer going to listen. Tonight would be the last time that Luca DeCarlo would control my life. It was time for me to take back my life. Pushing through the crowd to get to the other side of the club where the showroom was, I was getting whistled and winked at. Ugh, men were disgusting. Two guards were at the door, and even though they knew who I was, they wouldn't let me in.

"B. Come on. This isn't a place for you," Alfie said as he followed behind me.

"Shut it, Alfie. Get me in."

"No," Alfie shook his head. "There's probably naked women and other shit going on you shouldn't see."

"I'm so sick of people telling me what I should and shouldn't see or do. If you don't get me in there, I'll tell Luca about what you told me."

Shocked, Alfie replied, "We had a deal."

I roll my eyes, "Get a grip, Alfie."

Even though I would be told of this arranged marriage, Luca wouldn't take it well knowing Alfie spilled the beans to me behind his back. Alfie took a deep breath and shook his head in disapproval.

Nodding to the guards, "Let her in." Looking back to me, "I won't make the mistake of asking you for a favor again."

It stung to hear that. Alfie was like a little brother to me, but he didn't understand where I came from. I will deal with him later, but I needed to speak to my brother.

We entered the room; the lights were dim with blue LED lighting. There was a stage at one end of the room with a bar on the other end. The room wasn't big but had lots of seating. As I passed a few men getting lap dances, there was a secluded section that had seating around a little stage with a stripper pole in the center. On there was a woman half naked, twirling her body seductively around the pole. Seated was my brother talking to a man as they watched the woman.

Emilio was seated on the side, watching the woman on the pole. His suit jacket was removed, his top buttons undone, and his sleeves rolled up. He looked like his workday was over, and he was now enjoying the night. Looking at his exposed arms, I see they are tattooed. Just watching him casually sit there enjoying the view of the woman on the pole as smoke from cigars sifted through the air made me wish I was on that pole and that he was watching me. Without moving, his eyesight shifted to me and caught me staring at him. He leaned forward and caught Luca's attention. They exchanged a few words, and then Emilio quickly approached me.

"Bethany, what are you doing here?"

The scent of him hit me, and I felt weak. His shirt was untucked, and all I could think about was reliving one of the imaginary scenes I put together when touching myself.

"Bethany?" Emilio repeated my name, who knows how many times.

Eventually, I snap out of it. "I need to speak with Luca."

"Talk to him tomorrow."

"No. Now."

"I said tomorrow," he sounded upset.

"And I said now." I stood my ground.

Emilio grabbed me by the elbow and led me away from the secluded area.

"What is the issue?" he asked.

"I'm not marrying anyone," I stated as though it was Luca I was speaking to.

"What are you talking about?"

"I'm serious."

He took a deep breath, "Fucking Alfie."

"Don't blame Alfie. I'm not doing this anymore. Playing by Luca's rules and doing as he says."

Emilio seemed to get annoyed. "Like you have it so hard, sweetheart. You should be grateful instead of whining."

"I'm not whining."

"You didn't complain when he bought you that fancy condo looking over the Chicago River or the designer shoes and bags you have. Your brother has supported you since the day you graduated college. You agreed to this."

"I didn't agree to him dictating my life."

"Accepting the comfy life he gives you is agreeing without words."

"Well, I want to change that."

"Too late for that." Emilio stood tall while looking at me. "What is it that you want, Bethany? Your outbursts lately have been getting out of hand."

"Don't worry about me," I replied.

"Maybe you should pick up a hobby."

Insulted, "Maybe you should know your place and go get me brother."

"Watch your mouth."

This infuriated me. "Emilio– "

He stepped closer, "Bethany."

It shook a little fear into me when he stepped closer. "Get Luca."

Emilio stepped closer. There was a spark in his eyes—the kind where he was like an animal hunting their prey. Without fail, it lit me on fire. I tried to look away, but it was hard not to. Hell, I wanted to be hunted.

"I said no." With another step closer, he got close to my face.

I felt like I was panting for air at this point. "You can't keep me from speaking to my brother."

"You know exactly what I can do."

"Fine," I reply as I walk away.

If I want my brother's attention, I'll have to get it the hard way. Finding a pole surrounded by men, I approach them as I take off my leather jacket and toss it to the side with my purse. Making my way up the platform, I grab the pole like I know what I'm doing. Catching the attention of the men surrounding the platform as I spin around once, my hair swinging in the air, my body collides with another, and I get ripped off by Emilio. Tossing me over his shoulder, he stomps off as I kick and squirm for him to let me down. He barely seemed to struggle, no matter how hard I tried to get out of his grip.

Taking me back to the private room, he shouts to the few people there, "Get the fuck out. Now."

Everyone scattered without a fuss. Emilio threw me onto one of the sofas, which slammed into the wall.

"What is wrong with you?!" I shouted.

"With me?" Emilio huffed as he clenched his fists. "You've lost your mind."

I get to my feet and stand in front of him, "Fuck. You."

It seemed to be a natural reaction for him as he lifted his hand and pushed against my chest without much effort, causing me to fall back onto the sofa. "I'd tell you to go fuck yourself, but you'd probably put a show on for everyone while doing it."

Squinting my eyes in anger, I returned to my feet, although there wasn't much room since Emilio stood close to the sofa. "You wouldn't be able to stop me."

"Why are you testing my patience, Bethany?" he growled.

"I just wanted to speak to Luca."

"And what will that do for you, sweetheart? You think you can change his mind?"

"I can put up a good argument."

Emilio laughed in amusement. "I thought you understood your place. Your life is fated to be whatever Luca wants it to be."

Fated. No, that wasn't the deal. Luca promised to take care of me; I didn't expect him to use me as a bargaining tool. I felt like an idiot. My vision was becoming blurry. Not wanting to cry, I did my best not to blink. Trying to walk around him, Emilio blocked me with his arm and placed me in front of him again. I tried to push him, but he didn't move. Again, I try to walk around him, and he blocks me, but this time, he spins me around and pulls me to him.

With my back pressed against him, he whispers, "I can't change the situation, but I can make you forget it for the time being."

Chapter 11

Standing behind me, he wrapped one arm around the front of my torso, grabbing both wrists and holding them against my stomach. With his other hand on my chin, his thumb skimming my lips, then pulling down my lower lip. My breathing deepened as I let him drag his finger down my chin, skimming slowly down my neck until it reached the base where his entire palm rested.

The palm of his hand gripped the base of my neck. My insides were melting as I looked into his eyes and sensed all the danger behind them. His hand slid down my chest, and he pulled down my tube top, tracing my bra with his finger to the back hook. With one snap, the bra was undone and fell to the floor. It was quick, and my body reacted immediately.

With my breasts completely exposed, I kept my eyes on the wall in front of me that had a mirror to display what was happening in front of my eyes. I watch his free hand unbutton my pants, then unzip me, making his way under my panties. I deeply inhale when he places his hand over my lace underwear and pushed the fabric to the side to slide two of his thick fingers over my clit. I inhale sharply at how sensitive the area was to his touch.

"I want you to watch." His grip around my wrists was tight. "Understood?"

The words were caught in my throat, and I could not reply as he slid his fingers back and forth over the delicate area.

"Bethany, do you understand." He wasn't asking. He was commanding.

"Yes," I muttered.

The hand holding my wrists loosened, and he took them to my breasts. "I want you to get them as hard as you can."

I do as he pleases as we both watch through the mirror. He eyed me, touching my breasts and flicking my nipples until they were hard. His fingers rubbing on my clit were now wet, moving them further down he slid his fingers inside me. Emilio eyes lit up at the sound of a moan escaping my mouth.

"Harder," he demanded.

The harder I twisted my nipples, the faster his fingers slid in and out of me.

"Pull," he stated.

As I pulled on my nipples, he entered another finger inside me and shoved all three as far in as they could go, pulsing them quickly, no longer sliding them out. The build-up of an orgasm was growing rapidly. His thumb made its way to my clit, and the pressure tipped me over the edge. I let out a cry as my legs went numb. Emilio held me up, pressing his body against mine. His fingers were drenched with my cum and I watch him them into his mouth and pull them out leaving them now clean.

He grabbed my hair, pulling it as he spun me around to face him. I made sure my hardened nipples touched his chest through his shirt. With his free hand, he began to unbuckle his belt; I could see the excitement in his eyes as they darkened—the buckle clanking as he undid it made me breathe heavier. My chest lifted as I inhaled; I could feel my nipples dig further into his chest, and, in return, his grip on my hair tightened.

"MMM," the light moan escaped my lips.

Attempting to help him pull down his pants, Emilio swatted my hands away, so instead, I fell in front of him onto my knees, getting myself ready.

Watching him pull out his cock, it was just as intimidating as he was. With a wide girth, it looked like the veins were about to burst through the skin.

"Look at me," he demanded tightening the grip on my hair.

I did as I was told. He pushed his dick completely into my mouth while holding my head so that I couldn't pull away. It was a natural reaction to pull back as I began to choke, but this only made him go deeper down into my throat. My eyes widened and began to tear. I should be terrified that I'd die from suffocation, but in this moment, this was all I wanted. My mouth filled with saliva, and I could feel it sliding down my face. He was enjoying this as his thick cock took up my entire mouth. Keeping my eyes on Emilio, I could feel his hand brushing my cheek as though it would calm me down.

The realization on his face that he was being too aggressive had made him begin to withdraw from my mouth. I didn't know how much I needed this, and there was no need to pull back. My hands went to his thighs, and I pulled him back toward me, ramming his dick back down my throat. For the first time, it felt like I had total control, and it wouldn't slip through my fingers now.

"Jesus, Bethany!" he growled at my unexpected move.

Looking back down at me, his eyes were dark, completely dilated, full of lust. I dig my pink nails into his thighs to let him know this isn't over yet as I tighten my lips around the base of his shaft. Finally gaining his approval, both his hand clenched my hair again as I let him fuck my mouth numb. He was relentless in his thrusts, and I relished every moment as my eyes watered.

"I'm going to cum."

Before he could finish the words, I felt his hot semen burst out of him, shooting down my throat with excess spilling out of my mouth. Tears rolled down my cheek as I choked, but I refused for him to pull out until every drop of him went into my mouth. Emilio propped his arms forward onto the mirror on the wall for support, leaving a print. After swallowing every drop, I allow him to pull out. He watched as I licked the access cum that dribbled down my face until I got every last bit of it. His cock twitched in my face from excitement.

Grabbing my chin with his hand, "If you spill a word of this to anyone, I'll sow that pretty mouth of yours up."

Chapter 12

Waking up to thunder and lightning, I reach my sofa, wrapped in a comfy plush blanket. There was something beautiful in watching the city drowning in the rain. Relaxing to the sound of the raindrops outside, images of last night invade my mind. I would have thought it was just a dream. How could that have possibly happened? As I closed my eyes, my body tensed from the memory and was aching for more. A loud hit of thunder roared through the sky, causing me to open my eyes and return to my sofa.

Eventually, I made my way to the kitchen for some coffee, and I couldn't help but think how I would be able to look at Emilio the same way again. The thought of him sent waves of electricity through my body, so what would happen if I saw him in person? Would I be able to trust myself around him? His threat for me to keep my mouth shut was unwarranted. There was no chance I'd ever tell anyone—not even Natasha and Tiffany. The issue wasn't spilling what happened; it was that I wanted to do it again. I was in such a daze by what transpired between Emilio and I that I didn't even fuss about the arranged marriage when Luca dropped me home last night.

Emilio has been an asset to this family, not just to Luca. He made sure Rita's husband successfully took over the West side of Chicago as Captain, rushed Isabella to the hospital when she went into labor when she was home alone, unable to reach anyone else, he was there to help carry my father's casket and helped my mother plan the funeral. He was there for me, too. Emilio was someone we counted on during our tough times. For me, he was always there, getting me out of trouble.

"What have you gotten yourself into, Bethany?"

Emilio came as soon as I called. There was no one else I could think of to help with this situation better than he could, aside from my brother, but I was too scared to call Luca. Not wanting anyone to know, I swore to Emilio that I would do anything if this could stay between us.

"I didn't mean it," I was panicking. "I was trying to go back home."

"What if you got pulled over? You aren't even 21, and you're drunk."

Emilio puffed on a cigarette as he stood, looking at the dent in my car covered in blood. The smoke was a bright white against the night sky.

"He came out of nowhere." I sat on the side of the road feeling sick.

"Take a fucking cab next time."

Turning onto my hands and knees, I began to throw up violently. Emilio stepped away and made a phone call. When he walked back, he helped me to my feet.

"Don't vomit in my car."

"Where are we going?" I asked.

"I'm taking you home while I clean up this mess."

"Okay."

"And don't pull some shit like this again."

"You won't tell Luca, right?"

"No. Just don't let it happen again."

I swore that night I wouldn't drink and drive again. We left my damaged car and the dead body in the street. Unsure how this would all go under the radar, I knew it would be done when Emilio said he would handle something.

After a week of laying low, I walk into the kitchen with my mother, cooking a big dinner.

"Are we having company?" I asked.

"Your brother and Antonio are coming for dinner," she smiled. I was convinced that she loved Luca the most of all her children.

We all sat at the table when dinnertime arrived, eating and chatting.

"The mayor's son has gone missing. Have you seen the news, Luca?" my mother asked.

"I have. It's a shame."

"Is it?"

Our mother wasn't blind to who my brother was in this city.

"I have nothing to do with that," Luca stated.

A knock on the door put a confused look on our faces as we weren't expecting company.

"I'll get it," I said as I stood up.

When I opened the door, Emilio was lighting up a cigarette. I hadn't seen him since the night I called for his help.

"Good, you answered the door. I'm sure you heard who the person was from the other night."

I gulp, "I just found out."

"Eyes are looking in your brother's direction. I'm going to need to tell him."

In sheer panic, I begged, "Please. No. He's still getting over the Claire situation, and Antonio is adjusting from California to Chicago."

"I'm in a bind here, Bethany. He has to know what I did for you. We can't just ignore it."

"He'll hate me."

Emilio shook his head, "He'll forgive you. You're his sister."

My phone rang, and I saw it was none other than my brother. A chill rang through me. I hadn't thought about getting caught last night up until now. What if someone saw? Or the camera footage? Too nervous to pick up, I let it go to voicemail. While drinking my coffee, I nervously look at my phone, waiting for a voicemail notification, but instead, the phone rings again. The ringing stops. My eyes never leave the screen of my phone. It rings again, and now I'm in full panic mode. Luca never calls this many times unless he's pissed about something. This time, he left a voicemail.

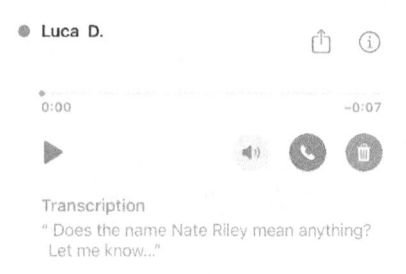

● Luca D.

0:00 —0:07

Transcription
" Does the name Nate Riley mean anything? Let me know..."

After hearing it, I breathed a sigh of relief. If Luca did find out, he would come pounding at my door and not call. I need to relax. Picking up my phone, I call Natasha.

"Hey, where have you been?" she asked.

I roll my eyes, "Busy getting things done for my brother."

"Isn't that what Emilio is there for?"

I laughed to myself; she didn't understand the roles of the lifestyle, no matter how many times I explained it.

"Things around the office. He hired a new developer."

"Okay, because Tiff swears you're mad about Alfie."

I had forgotten about them hooking up, but honestly, I didn't care.

I comment, "As long as she doesn't expect him to fall in love with her."

"Guess who came into my dad's bar a few nights ago?"

"Who?"

"Emilio."

I freeze at the sound of his name. Natasha is my best friend, but I wouldn't tell her about crossing the line with my brother's right-hand man. I didn't tell her much of anything when it came to my family.

"Was he alone?" I asked.

"Looks like he was on a date with some blonde, tall blonde chick who wore red lipstick. When I went to take her drink order, she didn't sound like she was from around here."

Hearing this made me jealous, but I had to play it off. "I'm surprised you didn't get more info. You're usually the nosy type."

"She wasn't very talkative. I only got her name when Alfie appeared and greeted her. The name Grace did not fit her personality."

"No one knows much about what Emilio does in his free time. I just assumed he didn't have any."

Natasha giggled, "How Emilio can be terrifying just as he is handsome is a mystery to me."

"Maybe that's the thrill of it," I replied, biting my lip as my mind went to last night.

"A man that screams danger is a thrill, Bethany Ann DeCarlo. I don't think your mother would approve," Natasha laughed.

"No, she wouldn't," I laugh with her. She wouldn't approve of my behavior last night, either.

"You always enjoyed a bit of trouble," there was ruffling on the phone, "I gotta go but call Tiff. Let her know you guys are on good terms."

As we got off the phone, I headed toward the bathroom to undress myself and take a long hot shower. There were a few errands I wanted to run today, but given the horrible weather, I opted to stay in and binge-watch Netflix.

As I walk out of the shower in a towel, I hear my phone buzz and see a few messages from Molly. She and Aria were looking to the area, reminding me of Luca's voicemail. I never called him back. When I did, I couldn't reach him.

Walking toward the living room to get my charger, I jumped out of my skin when I saw who was standing there.

"Bethany." Emilio stood there, his hands in his pockets and suit jacket unbuttoned.

CHAPTER 13

"What are you doing here?" I asked, although my first question should be how he got in here.

"Your brother was trying to reach you; I told him I would see where you were. You didn't answer the door, so I let myself in to make sure nothing was wrong."

Without moving further, I stood there clenching onto my towel in fear that if I caught a whiff of his scent, I would drop my towel on purpose. Emilio usually wore a nice clip with his suits, but today, there was no tie, and the top few buttons were undone. I liked this look on him, but I knew if I kept looking at him—I would misbehave.

Barely making eye contact, I replied, "You could have called or texted."

I could feel his eyes on me, "I thought we could talk. I prefer face-to-face."

My heart started pounding out my chest. I thought it was going to rip through my skin. "About last night?"

"It was a mistake. This time, poor judgment on my end."

Looking in his direction, I felt a pang of hurt by his words. No female wants to hear they are a regret.

"I wanted it," I replied.

"You understand that can't happen again."

I nod my head. He began walking towards me but not to me, clearly heading toward the door. This wasn't fair. Luca was going to marry me off without my consent—was I not allowed any happiness? Last night wouldn't happen again, and it tore me up inside so much that I made the boldest move. Instead of allowing him to walk past me, I slide over just in time. Emilio stopped short; the smell of mint and eucalyptus invaded my nose. We were face to face, and my line of vision was at his chin. Slowly, I lift my lids to look into his eyes.

"Just because I understand it can't happen again doesn't mean I don't want it to."

"Bethany. There are plenty of reasons why it shouldn't." The expression on his face told me he was angry with his furrowed brows and tightened mouth.

"You can lecture me on all those reasons. Repeat them as many times as you need to. But you haven't said that you don't want it to happen again."

"Don't push this."

"I'm not asking you to marry me, Emilio. I'm just asking you to fuck me."

"I get it," Emilio's voice was stern, "Sheltered princess gets off on having something she can't have. I don't need to be that guy."

"Are you saying that because you're afraid Luca will find out or because you aren't attracted to me?"

"Our fates are very different, Bethany. The worst Luca would do to you is lock you in the house. I'd be lucky if I get put in a box and put into a crematory chamber." He was angry, but somehow, instead of looking scary, he looked sexy.

"So you're afraid?"

"I'm not afraid to die, Bethany—I'm just not the kind of man to get mixed up with."

"You're a made-man, just like the rest."

"I'm very particular."

"And I'm willing."

Emilio took his hand and rubbed his chin. His brown eyes gleamed. Standing in silence as we both stare at one another, Emilio slowly walks toward me. "Why do you want this so bad?"

"Like you said—my life is fated. At least let me have some fun."

"And you chose with me?" he looks at me.

"I know you won't say a word, so there's no risk. We are just two people having fun." Letting go of the towel wrapped around me, it fell to the floor. "You can have me whenever, wherever you want, however you want."

Taking a step back so that he had a full view of my body that had streaks of water running down it from my wet hair, I took my hand and slowly dragged it across my collarbone. My fingers play on my skin as I drag them down over my breast, circling my semi-hard nipple and down my torso. I watch as the hunger in his eyes grows. A blast of thunder lights up the sky.

Without touching me, he examines my body with his eyes as he walks around me.

"Get on the sofa on your knees and put your hands on the wall."

I make my way over to the sofa placed against a glass window. It was raining even harder; the sky was grey, but that didn't ruin the mood. The leather sofa was soft on my knees, but the window behind the sofa was cool, and when I placed my hands on it, my nipples got harder. I can hear Emilio behind me unbuckling his belt and undoing his pants, which made my core a bit moist from the excitement. I never wanted something so badly. He grabs my hips tightly, sending a wave of excitement through my body. He pulls my hips back just enough with my knees spread apart as far as they can go as he positions himself behind me.

Grabbing my hair, he huskily says into my ear, "Don't cum until I say."

"Okay," I pant from the thrill of the situation.

Emilio spits, and his saliva drips down my crack toward my opening. Feeling the head of his cock at my entrance, before I could take a breath, he pounds forward, shoving himself entirely inside me at once, causing me to shout in pleasure. Without giving me any breathing space to adjust or accept his size, Emilio immediately begins to pump in and out of me aggressively.

My eyes widen in shock as I try to steady my hands on the wall as he ruthlessly slams into me. Unable to control myself from loudly moaning and panting in pleasure, I wasn't sure I would be able to hold out. Thunder ripped through the dark sky, lighting up the room.

"Don't you dare fucking cum, Bethany."

"I'm... I'm... trying." It was hard getting the words out.

Rain and thunder invade the sky as he continues to plunge into me. How the hell was I going to stop this oncoming orgasm building up by his relentless thrusts that had my body spiraling out of control? Feeling his hands slide up my back and grip my shoulders as he continues to pound in and out of me barbarically, I'm overwhelmed with pleasure. His hands tightly grip my shoulders like he was reaching his breaking point.

"Not yet," he reminded me.

With a final thrust slamming into me with a force that had me tearing in pleasure, Emilio let out a groan cumming inside of me. He remains still for a moment before pushing me forward so that my breasts are entirely against the window. Then he leans on my back, circling his hips deeply while still inside me. I was on the edge of glory as he slid a finger down the center of my core. Finally, he said the words I desperately needed to hear.

"Cum for me," he commands as he applies pressure on my clit.

Without delay, my body jerks as the orgasm rips through me. He keeps his body on mine as I twitch from the aftermath of the orgasm. Once my body relaxes, he peels himself off. Our skin sticky from sweat. I could feel him remove his cock from inside me, and I collapsed onto the sofa, watching him adjust himself as his semen was spilling out of me.

Once he had his belt buckled, he finally gave in, "Okay, Bethany. You win. But we play by my rules."

"Okay," I agreed as I looked up at him.

"Now go return your brother's call."

With that, Emilio left my condo while I lay me both stunned and satisfied.

Chapter 14

I woke up the next day refreshed and feeling alive. The office will be buzzing today, with everyone in to greet Aria. Walking into my office, I find a pile of paperwork I need to get through. Before I could even sit, Emilio was at my door.

"Aria should be here soon. Luca wants to see you in his office."

"Okay," I nod my head.

"Heads up, I told him you didn't return his calls because you found out about the engagement."

"Did he ask how?"

"He already knew that you knew."

Emilio walked off—not looking twice in my direction. He was good at this. Grabbing a notebook and pen, I go to my brother's office.

"Why did I need to send Emilio to you yesterday?" was his first question.

"You could have come yourself to tell me how you are marrying me off to a stranger."

"Emilio said he talked some sense into you." Luca leaned back on his chair. "Is that true?"

"Yes," I admitted. "He reminded me that I still had a voice even when told what to do."

"Hm. Maybe I should send him more often."

"Wait, how did you know that I knew?"

"Alfie came clean and told me what happened. How you made a deal in which you then threw in his face and threatened to use it against him."

"He did?" I was surprised.

"You keep up with kind of reputation, and no one will trust you to hold your word."

"I know. I let my emotions get the best of me."

Luca sat back in his chair. "This marriage is for the best, B, I promise."

"Not exactly sure how."

"Lucky for you, Emilio made a good point last night. So everything is placed on hold for now."

A burst of relief made me smile, "I should thank him." I got to my feet.

"Hold off on that. Alfie is already on thin ice with him. He wasn't thrilled that Alfie had blurted out the information confidentially. In the meantime, you go make amends with Alfie."

I place my hand on my hip, "Why do you entertain him?"

Luca shrugged, "I like the kid. He has potential."

"But Emilio doesn't seem to agree."

"Emilio isn't the one in charge."

Changing the subject, "What was your voicemail about?" I questioned.

"There was a large delivery of flowers sent to the penthouse to Aria from Nate Reilly."

"Okay?" I questioned, not understanding the issue.

"I called to see if you knew anything about him."

Luca appeared off today. What was going on with him?

"I know he is Aria's business partner. They are equal owners of the company. Molly didn't say much about the guy. But I guess if he's sending her flowers, they might be more than that."

This seemed to irritate my brother. "Find out what you can."

"Why does it matter?"

"I want to know who has any idea of the hotel's location and that Aria is staying there."

It was an odd response, but I let it go.

The day went well, considering everyone was on edge. Aria didn't seem phased at all being around here, which made me think either she was stupid, which it's clear she isn't, or she is just as good at bluffing as my brother, which seems to be the more likely option. I did as Luca wanted, being nice and trying to befriend her, but she wasn't easy to break. And as I promised Emilio, we barely spoke unless we needed to. Without flirting or giving any sign, it would never seem like something was going on between us.

On the other hand, Alfie made it impossible not to miss that he and the redhead had something going. He would wink at her throughout the day, and she would giggle anytime he passed. Was that normal behavior for people who work together in the same setting?

I needed to speak to Alfie and clear things up with him. If he confessed to Luca about what he did, he took his role seriously and didn't want anything held over his head. I should start respecting his life choices.

"Hey," I said as the end of the day approached, and he walked by. "Want to grab drinks after we get out?"

"No," Alfie replied simply and continued walking.

Stunned and insulted, I walk after him. When I catch up to him, I ask, "You're still mad?"

I did my best not to roll my eyes. Luca knew what had happened, so why couldn't he get over it?

"No."

I huffed. "Then why are you acting like this?"

"Like what, Bethany?"

"Oh, so I'm Bethany now?"

"That's your name, isn't it?"

Getting fed up, I pick up my pace and cut him off by standing before him. "What is your deal, Alfie? Should I call you Alfred now since you want to get all formal on me?"

"Do what you want."

He tried to walk around me, but I cut him off again.

"Hey, look. I'm sorry. I was upset and wanted to speak to my brother."

"That's the thing, Bethany, you get upset and act out. Even with a meeting going on, you still insisted on seeing Luca. You act like a brat whenever you don't get your way."

"Excuse me?"

"You heard me, Bethany." Stepping to the side, he manages to get around me this time.

Turning in his direction, "So you're just going to be mad at me forever?"

Alfie stopped, turned around, and walked toward me again. He must have gotten taller, or maybe he just stood taller, but there was something different about him.

"No, Bethany. I'm not mad." Alfie put a hand in his pocket while the other pointed to me. "I should thank you. I talked with Luca after I confessed what I did. He was upset, but then we discussed what kind of man I wanted to be and how my actions would reflect that. Luca gave me some good insight. So I owe it to you."

"Okay, so my brother gave you a pass and gave you good advice. It all worked out for the best. And like you said, you have me to thank."

Alfie smiled and nodded his head. "That doesn't mean you get a pass."

"I want to make things right."

"Then you're going to have to prove your worth of that opportunity."

"Pretty ballsy coming from someone your rank."

Alfie smirked, "Didn't Luca tell you to play nice?"

Taken back by his response, his message was very clear. Alfie was going to use Luca against me. Since Luca took a liking to him, Alfie knew he could vent to Luca about me so I would get scolded.

"You're playing with fire," I hit back.

"I am the fire."

I watch Alfie walk away. He made it clear what kind of man he was looking to be. He may not have DeCarlo blood running through his veins, but he was sure to start acting like it.

Chapter 15

Getting to Thursday was long, and I felt like I was going crazy. Emilio and my brother weren't in the office this week, which I knew, but I didn't expect to be pining over when Emilio would reach out to me. If he did come to the office, his main focus was Aria, which made me jealous. Flings weren't my thing; I only ever had relationships. Was this how it works?

"Hey, Bethany!" Molly was a bit too happy-go-lucky for me, but I tried to be nice. "It's ladies' night. Want to go out?"

"No Alfie tonight?"

She shook her head, "He's been distant lately."

"Okay. Let's go to Timmy's. A friend of mine bartends there."

"I'll ask Aria if she wants to join. She's been working nonstop since we got here."

I highly doubt Aria would agree to ladies' night with two younger ladies, but I wasn't going to crush Molly's heart. "I'll come pick you up at the hotel."

It was around 11 pm when Tiffany and I got to the Lagos hotel. Knowing that Luca was here, I took a shot that Emilio would be around as well, so I suggested we have a drink at the lounge before we headed out. Making sure I wore something that would catch his eye, I strut my stuff into the building wearing a skin-tight peach halter tulle draped dress almost see-through that was low cut paired with cream-red bottoms. While in the lobby, we see Alfie with his arm wrapped around another girl, pulling her into him. She giggled as he was whispering in her ear. I shouldn't care what he does or with whom, but Molly was sweet, and any girl whose heart has been broken knows how it changes your perspective of men forever.

Tiffany also saw Alfie and her body tensed. "This is awkward."

I laugh, "You didn't think of that before you guys did the deed."

Rolling her eyes, "Please don't hang that over my head."

"Go grab us a round; I'll be there in a second."

As Tiffany headed towards the lounge, I walked toward Alfie. He saw me coming but didn't seem to care as he continued to whisper into the girl's ear, making her giggle.

"Alfie." I stood in front of them with my arms crossed against my chest.

"Bethany," Alfie replied.

Trying not to appear bothered, I asked, "Can I have a word?"

"You can speak right here."

This got on my nerves. He must still respect me if he wants to become a certain kind of man. I'm the DeCarlo here, not him. Glaring at him, Alfie finally gave in.

"Why don't you grab us a drink," he told the girl.

"Okay," she smiled.

As she walked away, Alfie slapped her ass. Who the hell was this? The girl giggled even more as she walked away with a big smile.

"Seriously?" I asked Alfie.

"What's the problem?" Alfie shot back.

"I thought you and Molly were a thing."

"We are. When I want. Tonight, I don't want to be a thing."

"All week, you haven't wanted to be a thing. What's wrong with you?"

"What the hell do you care anyhow?"

I huff. "You know what kind of man you want to be, but you don't need to be a prick."

"It works well for Emilio." Alfie had a sly smile on his face.

"That's the kind of man you want to be?"

"A womanizer," he replied, "Seems to be working well for him so far."

I was just about ready to slap him when Tiffany joined us. "Hey, your brother is in there with Aria. Not sure if you wanted to go in still. No one else is in there except them and Emilio with some woman."

"Why don't we just wait for Molly outside?" I suggest.

"Okay," Tiffany nodded.

"Hey Tiff," Alfie voiced.

"Hey Alfie," Tiffany blushed.

"I'll meet you out there," I tell her.

Once gone, I turn my focus back to Alfie. "Be whatever you want, but don't be that guy. Molly is a good girl. Don't be the asshole that turns her into a bitch."

As I walk away, passing the entrance to the lounge, I look in to see if I can spot Emilio with the woman. I wondered if it was the blonde that Natasha saw. Luca and Aria looked cozy at the bar, but no Emilio in sight. As I walk outside, I see Tiffany waiting there. I walk past the pillar outside the door into a puff of smoke.

Coughing, I look to see who would be rude enough to do such a thing. "What the hell!"

"Bethany." The sound of my name on his lips made me melt.

I made eye contact with Emilio, who was leaning against the pillar. His eyes look at me up and down as he pushes himself off the pillar and walks to me.

"What are you doing here?," he asked.

"Picking up Molly for ladies' night."

"Where to?"

"Timmy's."

"Have fun then."

Disappointed, I smile and nod my head. Was that it? No, see you later. Before I could walk away, a woman wrapped herself around him. She kissed his neck and whispered something into his ear. Despite this, Emilio remained looking at me.

"Have a good night," I fake a smile and walk away.

Furious that he didn't even care how I felt, I was livid. Molly came out just as I got to Tiffany. I didn't say anything during the entire car ride as Tiffany and Molly chatted. Natasha was at the bar, and I immediately started taking shot after shot.

"Whoa, slow down," Natasha urged, "What's gotten into you?"

"I need to get laid," I blurt out.

"Well, there are tons of good-looking men here. Take your pick."

I scoured the room, but no one caught my eye. Not the same way Emilio has been. I needed something more—that thrill. And nothing here was thrilling. What was going on with me? Did he have me this dickmatized? Molly and Tiffany were dancing the night away, but I sat myself by the bar.

"Bethany Ann DeCarlo."

I turned to see an unpleasant, familiar face that calling me by my full name.

Rolling my eyes, "Declan Connor. To what do I owe the pleasure?" the sarcasm spilled out of my mouth.

"You are looking fine as ever," he traced his finger along my shoulder.

I grab his finger and remove it from my skin. "You know better than to do that."

A sly smirk crossed his face. "I don't see anyone here to save you. Surprised you are left alone. A pretty thing like you."

A chill ran up my spine; I cursed internally at myself. All the whining I do about being followed and not having any independence went right out the window during moments like this.

"Get off me!" I pushed and kicked.
"Oh, come on. You know you want it."
"Cian! Stop."
"Please," I begged politely as I closed my eyes.

The more I seemed to push him away, the harder it was to get him off of me. Putting all his body weight on me, it wasn't easy to move. He managed to rip my stockings—I have begged my mother to get me. They had rhinestones scattered throughout and paired nicely with a black and white plaid skirt and booties. Managing to rip through my underwear, I was on the verge of tears as I felt I had no other choice but to give in. He is my boyfriend, so why say no? Granted, I'm a virgin, and this wasn't how I wanted it to happen, but fighting this was useless. I wasn't going to win, and it was better to have said I wanted this than to lose the battle. I'd end up a victim, and the DeCarlo's are not victims.

Right as I talked myself into going through with this, the weight of Cian's body lightened. My eyes open to see Emilio tossing him onto the ground, then proceeding to beat him to a bloody pulp. Too stunned to speak, I remained frozen.

"Take him to the box," Emilio shouted to one of the other men.

That was the last day anyone took advantage of me again.

It was the first of many times Emilio came to my rescue. I've heard rumors as to what happened to Cian. He was put in the box. The box was code for the torture chamber. Rumor has it that Cian was put in the box, tied up, and eaten alive by rats.

"I didn't think you'd be stupid enough to approach me." I wasn't the same scared 16-year-old. Cian was Declan's brother. He didn't even deserve me facing him, so I sat looking at the liquor wall behind the bar.

Declan laughed it off. "I heard Casper took a job in Wyoming."

"Good for him." I was uninterested, but he wasn't getting the hint.

"I also heard you'll be Mrs. Appollo soon. Is it true?"

This caught my attention, causing me to turn my head toward him. "I didn't know you were such a gossip queen."

Leaning in close, he seemed happy to relay, "I hear one of them beat his wife to death because she didn't make the bed, and the other is even more sadistic."

My body tensed. He was trying to get under my skin—the problem was that it was working. Declan walked away with a smile, knowing his words got me shook. There's no way Luca would allow this union if the man was that awful. The walls were closing in on me and I took a deep breath. Waving to the bartender, I order another shot.

"B, you should calm down." Natasha approached me as I down the tequila.

"I'm going to head home after this one," I assured her.

"What did Declan say? Are you okay?"

"I'm fine."

After taking another shot, I stumbled out of the bar, but I wasn't looking to go home. Instead, I pull out the business card from the sex party that I kept stashed in my purse at all times. Holding it already sent electric waves through my body.

There was a party tonight, and I wasn't going to miss it.

Chapter 16

Surprisingly, this party was held at the chic Legacy Hotel in a suite inaccessible for public use. The suite aesthetic was as though it were designed specifically for these kinds of events. With a large floor area and two staircases leading up to a second floor of private rooms, it felt like I entered a forbidden paradise. Unlike the other parties I've been to, the lights were all on. You could make out everyone's face and no one was shy about it.

At the door, I was told clothing was optional, but even with liquor running inside me, I was still too timid. My dress was tight, so there was no need to wear a bra. If I took the dress off, I'd only be in my underwear, and I wasn't brave enough. Both men and women eyed me as I walked by, some licking their lips. For such an open-lit space, there were people all over the place filling out their sexual desires so unafraid. I wasn't necessarily watching their acts but admiring their courage in expressing themselves so openly.

I found myself walking up one of the flights of stairs. At the top, there was a sign with arrows. One arrow pointed in one direction that read orgies while the other arrow pointed in the direction that read audience. Curious to see what the audience side meant, I walked down the hall where each room had an open door where people came in and out. Approaching the first room, a group watched two women devour each other. Not into watching, I head to the next room. There was loud panting as I entered the space. People softly whispering to each other.

"Ugh, I'd give anything to be her right now," a woman says to another.

I was going toward the center, where people glued their eyes on a man and a woman. She was on her back, propped up onto her elbows with her head tilted back as she moaned in pleasure. The man was on his knees with his face planted right onto her core. When the woman pulled her head back to watch the man, I recognized who she was. Hearing her scream, I tried to remember where I had seen her before. I step forward to get a better view but I was so distracted by their performance to focus. I watched the man bite her, eat her, swallow her, all while never taking his eyes off her.

I took in his every move. Watching him get off his knees and enter inside of her, he didn't even bother wiping his mouth wet with her juices. He held onto her waist, ramming himself inside her fast and strong with every pulsating movement. He looked as though he was going to break her. Then, in a swift movement, he flipped her on her hands and knees. Cupping her breast, he kissed her shoulder. Unable to take my eyes off of them, I stood there, feeling the moisture build between my legs.

A man stood beside me, gaining my attention. "Do you want some?"

I bit my bottom lip as the man waited for my answer. In desperation for sexual release, I nod my head. He motions for me to follow him into an empty room with a bed on a platform set up like a stage. Throwing me onto the bed, he looks down at me.

The man grinned in excitement. "Let's role play."

"What do you have in mind?"

The first thing he did was rip my dress off.

In a matter of minutes, a few people walk into the room. By then, I was completely naked, my face down and ass up with the man's tongue swirling inside me. Everything about this was outside my comfort zone, but the feeling was too good to make it stop. Rather than focus on the room of people, I close my eyes and bury my face into the mattress as I let out my cries of pleasure. A pinch of pain jolts through me as the man slaps my bare ass causing me to lift my head. The room was full of people watching me on all fours as he enters his cock inside of me. The man barely lasted 60 seconds. Strangers are watching as the man climaxes and cums all over my back. My body falls forward as he lets go of me. The regret sets in immediately.

I hear the room empty, and eventually, I sit up. With guilt pitted deep in my stomach, I get dressed and walked as fast as my feet could. I didn't stop until I was outside the hotel. By the time I exited the doors, that guilt plummeted into anger. All I wanted was Emilio's attention, and not getting it led me to this.

The smell of the air weighed heavily, and the lack of people outside somehow made me feel abandoned. As I approach the taxi pickup area, my phone rings. My spirit lifted for a moment, thinking that it was Emilio—how I craved his attention now more than ever made no sense. But it wasn't Emilio who was calling and as quickly as my spirit rose, it quickly dropped.

"What do you want, Alfie?" I answered.

"Where are you?"

"Why?" the annoyance in my voice was evident.

"Molly drunk dialed me. I came to pick her up; she said you left. Are you okay?"

I roll my eyes as I get into one of the cabs. "I'm fine."

"You don't sound fine."

"Why would it matter to you anyway?" I spat out before telling the driver my address.

"I care, that's why."

"Sure," I laugh.

"Come on, B."

"We are back to B now. I prefer you calling me Bethany."

Alfie huffed. "You are right," he confessed, "I don't need to act a certain way to be the man I want to be. It's a thin line, and I'm just trying to find my footing."

"Okay," I replied, just wanting to go home. Alfie's behavior was the last thing I cared about right now.

"Can you tell me where you are? Please?"

"Just leaving the Legacy Hotel," I replied.

"What are you doing there?"

"Private party."

"I'm coming."

"I'm in a taxi already," I huffed.

Alfie finally got off the phone with me once he knew I was taken safely back to my condo. The first thing I did when I walked through my door was scrub my body clean in the shower.

Chapter 17

I woke up to a text from Luca saying the office would be closed for observation and to let the staff know. Observation? What was being observed? There must be something big my brother has planned today, and he wants the building cleared. Thinking of something on the spot, I sent a blast e-mail letting everyone know the office would be closed, only to get hit with questions I didn't have answers to. Doing my best to give vague answers, I got frustrated and called Luca directly, but he didn't answer. No one would question Luca if he sent that out himself. The next best option was Emilio, but I wasn't going to reach out to him; plus, if they were in the middle of something, I shouldn't be interrupting.

"What is going on?" I asked Alfie when he answered my call.

"Good morning to you, too."

"Sorry," I huffed, "I'm getting pushback from a few people needing to log into the system to get a few things done today. Luca won't answer."

"He's not going to. He's spending the day with Aria."

"Why would they be working but close down the office?"

"Who said they are working?"

"So what the hell are they doing?"

"For a smart girl, B, sometimes things go over your head."

I paused for a moment, and then it hit me. "You got to be kidding me. How do you know?"

"Emilio has me following them to make sure things run smoothly. This is my shot to prove myself."

"So what is Emilio doing then?"

"Probably waiting for me to fuck up and boast about it. The guy hates me."

As Alfie was speaking, I got another call. To my surprise, it was Emilio. A jolt of joy shot through me, and I quickly got off the phone with Alfie to answer Emilio's call.

"Hello," I casually answered, even though my stomach was in knots.

"Get your ass here."

I gulp. Did I mishear him? "Where?"

"My place."

"You weren't satisfied last night? That woman was all over you."

"No one ever told you to never believe anything you hear and only half of what you see?"

I found myself in front of Emilio's door. Closing my eyes as though it would give me confidence, I stood there for a while before I knocked on the door. His condo had a doorbell, but I was too nervous I would seem desperate to use it. No answer. I should be making him grovel but I'm too weak for that.

The door opens, and there he stands shirtless, wearing sweatpants that hung on his hips, fully exposing his v-cut. Measuring me with his eyes while his face showed no emotion, he leaned against the door frame. He looked like a mix of sex and power. I've always seen Emilio perfectly put together with his hair nicely combed back. But I was in his personal space now with his undone, dirty blonde hair that fell onto his forehead.

"Come in," he said, teetering on the edge of seduction.

I follow him into his kitchen. His entire back was covered in a large mural skull tattoo. The look gave him a completely different tone—like he wasn't scared to bury you in the backyard. Taking my focus away from his body, I observe his place which wasn't what I expected, although I wasn't sure what to expect from him. The color scheme was grey, white, and cream.

"Coffee?" he asked, breaking the awkwardness.

"Okay."

As he made a pot of coffee, I couldn't take my eyes off him. Looking at his back as his muscles flexed with each movement, I started breathing heavier and needed to look away. No one has ever set foot in his condo; I doubt even Luca. It was as though I unlocked a secret code. The layout of the condo was an open concept. Walking around the place, I look at the art on the walls.

"I didn't take you as an art fanatic."

"I have my interests," he voiced from the kitchen.

There was one piece that caught my eye. It was in the dining room—DaVinci's mural of The Last Supper painted onto the stone wall to replicate the original. The center of the room had a long, dark wooden slab table with a chandelier that hung over it.

"For someone from the South Side, you've grown accustomed to nice things," I comment.

"When life changes, you need to keep up with it."

I saw him looking at me as he leaned against the wall with his shoulder.

"What made you call me over?" I asked.

"You think showing up in that dress last night wouldn't get my attention?"

"Did it?"

"The only time you should wear something like that is when you see me. No other pair of eyes should see what I see."

Thinking back to last night I place my hand on my hip, "And if they do?"

He smirked, "I'll rip their eyes out myself."

Getting bored as we stared at one another, Emilio pushed himself off the wall and walked away. Confused and unsure of what was going on, I walked in the direction he went. Emilio turns down a hall and into a room, all without checking if I was following.

My feet took me to the door opening, which led into his bedroom. It was minimal, only containing a bed with two nightstands on each side. The black bed frame is made from kiln-dried solid mahogany with intricate foliage, scroll and fretwork carvings, and molded accents. It had a sense of Greek-Roman inspiration, and the headboard had a carving in the center with a Gothic gargoyle face.

Watching him, he stops at the edge of the bedframe and removes his pants before lying down on the mattress. He was completely naked. Stuck on whether he didn't wear undergarments in general or this was an at-home thing, I stood in shock at the door entrance.

"If you want it, Bethany, you're going to have to come get it."

Chapter 18

"If you want it, Bethany, you're going to have to come get it."

I badly wanted this, so why am I completely frozen in place? As he lay on the bed with his hands behind his head, just observing me, my eyes glided down his body like it was the first time I saw a naked man. His manhood wasn't fully hard, but it lay against his leg. I knew he was thick but didn't realize how big he was. How did that fit inside of me?

My legs began to move toward the bed as I removed my clothes. His usual cold and piercing stare was replaced with a savage and lust-filled look. Off went my shirt, then my bra.

"Leave the heels on," Emilio said. "And take down your hair."

Removing my shorts and underwear, my final four steps had me standing at the edge of the bed, looking down at Emilio, who remained relaxed. My heart was beating out of my chest, and I was slightly terrified. Pulling my hair tie, I let my hair fall out of the ponytail and cascade down my body—the ends hitting right under my breasts. Climbing onto the bed, I tossed my leg over his body so that I sat straddling him. His cock was right under my ass, and I felt it getting tense, which in return made my body react. Thrusting his pelvis up, he was encouraging me to move up. Wiggling a bit forward, I see a smile cross his face.

"I want you to sit on my face."

His forwardness shouldn't be surprising, but I felt like a schoolgirl being told to do something scandalous. Encouraging me by thrusting his hips again, I make my way toward his head. When I reach his chest, his hands grab my thighs, lifting me and placing me directly on his mouth. The wetness of his tongue inside of me had me grab onto the headboard face to face with the carved gargoyle. Swerving his tongue and sucking on me felt sensational. His hands grasping my bare ass, encouraged me to begin moving so that I would grind onto his face. When I was moving on my own without his control, he continued eating me out without stopping for a moment. I began moaning and when I thought I was going to cum, he sat up, and tossed me off of him straight onto his cock then lay back down onto his back.

I shout out, "Fuck!"

Having no control, I felt it all. The thickness of his cock squeezing into my opening, the length of his cock hitting my cervix, and his hands gripping my hips as he lifted me and slammed me back down onto him as he thrust upward had me spiraling into madness. Unable to catch my breath for a second, Emilio held me down as he repeatedly slammed his cock inside me. My pussy clenches around his solid hard cock throbbing inside of me. The sound of our skin slapping together and my tits bouncing around—it must have looked like a porno, but I was enjoying every damn second. Even when I came, he was relentless until he hit his climax. With one final slam of our bodies, Emilio held me down as he came inside of me. I was breathless and fell forward onto the headboard with my hands holding me up for support. Emilio laid still with his eyes closed.

Sitting up, I look down at him as he opens his eyes. Placing his hands behind his head, he looked at me as though he was admiring a piece of art while I remained seated on top of him with my hands on his chest.

"Did you enjoy yourself?"

"Yes," I admitted.

"Was it better than what you had last night?"

My eyes widened. How did he know? Looking away, embarrassed, "How did you know?"

"Who did you think made Alfie call you?" Emilio hoisted his hip to get my attention, forcing me to look at him again.

"Do you think less of me for it?"

"Sweetheart, I'm the last person to cast the first stone."

"Bible reference. Didn't take you as a religious man."

Emilio laughed. "My relationship with God is complicated."

Thinking back to his earlier comment about another pair of eyes looking at me. I couldn't help but ask.

"The man .. is he... okay?"

Emilio took a deep breath, "He's alive if that's what you're asking."

"I made a stupid compulsive choice yet pretty sure half of Chicago's women have been in your bed."

"I'm insulted you think it's only half," Emilio jokingly said.

I nudge him, "The double standard isn't fair."

It was no surprise Emilio lived the bachelor life, but to hear him confirm it made me feel uncomfortable, which he noticed. "I'm very particular, Bethany. Just because I have different women on my arm doesn't mean I'm sleeping with them."

"No?"

He smirked, "Well... not all of them."

Feeling insecure, "Do I satisfy you?"

"Shouldn't I be the one asking you that?," quickly lifting his hip then down to remind me that he was still inside me as he wanted an answer.

"I don't mind only having you but ... am I enough?"

"Guys will always get off, women don't," Emilio replied, "So it's the man's job to make sure she gets off."

He wasn't wrong but keeping a man's attention wasn't easy. I've heard guys talking before about the women they sleep with and which they prefer more.

"I just don't want you to hold back."

Unsure he trusted his instinct, he lay there for a moment. He shot out his arm toward me, grabbing my neck firmly as I was still straddling him. His cock twitched inside me. His look was menacing, which terrified me as much as it excited me. He lay there effortlessly, just gazing at me when suddenly he pulled me toward him; my hands landed on his chest for support. Our lips almost touched, and I could feel him getting hard again. This was a first for me. Feeling him growing while still inside me spiked my arousal once again.

Desperate for a kiss, Emilio just continued to tease me. The palm of his hand against my throat as his fingers almost wrapped completely around my neck remained in a tight hold. Something I never thought I'd enjoy. Attempting to make the move, quenching my thirst for our lips to touch, Emilio ensured it was impossible. His hold on my neck dictated my movement.

His eyes lit up, "I'm going to claim every inch of you."

Rolling over, with his hand unremoved from my throat, he lay pressed onto my body. His cock was rock solid, still fully inside of me. Slowly removing it, our cum came dripping out of my core. I feel fingers entering inside of me, pushing the juices back in. His fingers steadily entered in and out of me; Emilio continued trailing kisses down my neck and onto my chest. He plops a breast into his mouth and takes a suck before biting down on my nipple.

The shot of pain made me arch my back and sharply inhale. It was pleasurable just as it was painful, and I lived for it. I watch as he pulls on my nipple, letting it scrape against his teeth until it plops out as his grip around my neck tightens. Emilio continued making his way down my body; the hand on my neck loosened and made its way to my other breast, tugging relentlessly. Emilio made his way to my pussy and dived right in, replacing his fingers with his tongue.

The same fingers that were inside me now entered my rectum, causing me to lift my pelvis in reaction, but Emilio just pushed me back down into the bed. The hand on my breast made its way to my clit, and he worked my lower region all at once—every weak spot hit. I was practically screaming in pleasure. I've never had any anal pleasure before, it always seemed daunting, but I was enjoying this. His fingers stretch out my tight hole as gently as possible. My entire body was reacting, and I knew this orgasm was going to be intense. But rather than let me finish, Emilio flipped me onto my stomach and lifted my hips so that my ass was up in the air. His hands open my ass cheeks, and he spits right into my crack. The wetness dripped down toward my anus as his thumb rubbed the spit around and into it. While on his knees, he grabbed my hair so that my back was pressed onto his chest. His erection at my hole made me shiver.

"Have you before?" he asked.

"No," I whisper.

I knew what was going to happen and held my breath, waiting for the impact. Emilio has been aggressive, but he eased inside my butthole. Holding back from yelping, I took quick breaths until he was fully inside. He inhaled as though trying to contain himself as his cock twitched inside. Slowly, he thrust in and out of me. He kept his hand entangled in my hair, gripping hard and distracting me from the other pain. His other hand made its way to my clit, and he began to rub in rhyme to his thrusting. Suddenly the pain turned into pleasure, and once I began moaning, Emilio's cock throbbed again. I was sure he was ready to cum.

"It's okay," I encouraged knowing he was trying to remain gentle.

Pushing me down so I was on my hands and knees, he grabbed my hips and began pounding his cock into me. With a few aggressive strokes, he lets out a growl, and his hot semen shoots inside. We fall onto the bed, with him onto me. As I remain on my stomach, Emilio lays on his back beside me.

A sexy smirk crossed his face, "I think I'll keep you," then places his lips onto my shoulder for a kiss.

We must have dozed off. The sound of a phone ringing wakes us. Emilio reaches onto the nightstand to answer it. He didn't say much, just asked, "When?" "Where?" and "Let me know when he leaves."

Jumping out of bed, he turns to me. "What do you know about a Nate Reilly?"

I shrug. "He works with Aria."

"I know they are business partners, but I want to know if there's more to it. Do me a favor—find out anything and everything."

Sitting up, I nod my head. "What's the problem?"

"He just showed up to the Lagos."

"Why is that a problem?"

"Just odd, she spends the day with your brother, and then this guy shows up."

Shrugging my shoulders, "I'm not making the connection."

"Just find out whether Aria's messing around with the guy."

Emilio walks out of the room, and I hear him mumbling something to someone on the phone. When he walks back in, he heads straight toward me, grabs my ankle, and pulls me to the end of the bed toward him.

I squeal when he tosses me over his shoulder. "What are you doing?"

"Taking a shower, and I want the imprint of your ass cheeks on the glass."

I wake up beside Emilio, who sleeps comfortably on his stomach, facing away from me. It shouldn't be surprising he wasn't a cuddler, but maybe that's how flings work. Getting up to use the restroom, I look myself in the mirror naked. My nipples were purple, and I had bite marks on my body strategically placed where clothing normally covers. When I returned to the bedroom, Emilio was seated in bed, looking at his phone.

"Everything okay?" I asked.

He got out of bed. "I need to go."

Chapter 19

While driving back to my place, my phone rings. When I see it, it is Luca, my body tenses.

"Get to my house. Now."

His demand made me nervous.

"Sure," I reply, "You sound on edge."

"Just get here, Bethany."

My brother only said my full name when he was angry, and although he didn't allude to anything specific, I couldn't help but feel like I got caught. The entire ride, my stomach was in knots. While pulling into his driveway, I see Emilio's car. My heart started pounding. Seeing his car here was never surprising, but I was concerned this time.

"Ms. DeCarlo," the butler addressed me. "Your brother is in his office waiting for you."

I walk away before remembering Luca scolding me for my lack of sympathy toward the house's staff. I didn't want him to add this to the list if he was upset with me.

"Thanks," I reply, wishing I could remember his name.

I could hear my brother speaking as I walked toward the wing of the house that was forbidden to be in unless Luca asked for you.

"Go down there and remind her whose city she is in," Luca demanded.

"Will do."

"And next time, Emilio, I should get calls with resolutions, not problems."

"I'll make sure of it," Emilio assured him. "I suggest we do something about Alfie."

I listened closely to hear what they were talking about. What could Emilio mean by doing something about Alfie?

"I'm not getting rid of him."

Emilio huffed, "Luca, I'm not sure why you have this attachment to this kid. He owes you nothing."

"It's none of your concern, E."

They only addressed themselves this casually behind closed doors. Over the years, they have grown close. I'd even go as far as to say they were friends.

"It is my concern," Emilio replied. "You take this orphan under your wing, and then you have me look after him like he's one of our own."

"He is."

"He was initiated into the family after a damn week of knowing him, Luca."

"I don't need to explain anything to you. You work for me, and if I tell you to do something, I expect it done without pushback."

Even though I wasn't in the room, I felt the tension. I knock before walking in.

"Hi," I smile, and I enter the room.

I find Luca and Emilio standing facing each other with a drink in hand.

"A bit early to drink," I commented.

"It's been a rough morning," Luca stated.

I shot Emilio a questioning look, but he turned away and poured more liquor into his cup. He was avoiding me.

Luca went on. "Bethany, Gabe Appollo wants a wedding within the week."

My stomach dropped. "That's extremely last minute."

"It's not ideal, but I can't push it off."

I laugh, "Yes, you can. You're Luca DeCarlo."

Walking toward the liquor stand, Luca hands his glass to Emilio for a refill. "Something has come up."

"Like what?" I huffed.

"Nothing for you to be concerned about."

"Nothing to be concerned about?!" I cross my arms at my chest. "You're so quick to marry me off. What could be so important to override that?"

Just as I finished saying that, there was a knock at the door.

"Come in," Luca shouted.

Alfie steps in. "You wanted to see me?"

"Yes," Luca replied. "You're going to California."

The news took back both Alfie and me.

"Have I done something wrong?" Alfie asked.

"No," Luca replied, "Emilio told me you've become quite the asset."

Emilio poured a drink into a glass and gave it to Alfie as he joined our circle. Alfie seemed skeptical initially taking it but took the cup and waited to hear more.

Luca continued, "My uncle Neil is looking to retire. His position will be open for the taking. I think you would be a good fit."

"I prefer being in Chicago," Alfie replied.

"You'll learn a lot from Neil. Give it a shot; we can revisit the conversation if you still don't like it after the year ends."

As though there were no other answers, Alfie replied, "Whatever you want, Luca."

"You'll catch a flight with Aria," Emilio added. "You leave in an hour."

"Go pack a few things; anything else you need, you can get while you are there," Luca said.

Alfie gulped his drink and smiled before walking out.

I ask my brother, "You're sending Alfie to look after Aria?"

"No," Luca replied, "Like I said, Neil will be showing him the ropes out there."

"I'm sure the redhead will love that," I comment.

"The redhead stays in Chicago."

The confusion was written on my face. Luca shot Emilio a look to let him fill in the blanks.

Emilio cleared his throat, "The redhead is keeping tabs on Aria and on us to report it back to her brother in New York. Keeping her here will let them think they still have an upper hand."

I nod my head even though none of this makes sense to me.

"Wear something nice tonight," Luca said.

"Where are we going?" I asked.

"You have dinner with your fiancé."

Chapter 20

I walked into Slava, one of Chicago's upscale restaurants, and was escorted to a table surrounded by people in the center of the dining area. Wearing my sleeveless charmeuse sheath dress with bluebell print with silk satin lining, a straight neckline that tied around the neck paired with black, red bottoms, I was looking to make a decent impression. It was playful but elegant. Luca was supposed to accompany me, but Gabe wanted a one-on-one only. It was odd my brother agreed to it.

"Bethany," he pulled out my chair.

He was about my height, with a five o'clock shadow, dark hair, and dark brown eyes. He wasn't bad-looking but not attractive enough for anyone to believe I'd want this marriage willingly. Gabe had to be in his mid 40s.

"Gabe," I smile. "Nice to finally meet you."

Once seated, Gabe sat right next to me fairly close, which I found odd, being it was a round table.

"I heard you were beautiful, but that was an understatement," he smiled, and I felt his hand on my knee under the table.

"Thank you," I smile and gently push his hand off me.

The waiter came to announce their specials and take our order.

"We'll have a bottle of wine," Gabe ordered. "I'll have the tomahawk steak well done, and she will have the salmon salad."

I look up from the menu, trying to understand. Did he order for me?

I smile at the waiter, saying, "I'll have the 6lb Maine Lobster."

I didn't mind lobster; I just chose the most expensive item on the menu to be spiteful.

Gabe smiles, "Honey, we are getting married in a few days. Maybe you should go light on your meal."

The waiter looked uncomfortable and awkwardly stood there.

"I'm hungry tonight." I turn to the waiter to kindly dismiss him, "Thank you."

Gabe looked like he was holding back as his eye seemed to twitch. "Don't tell me you plan to lose your figure once married. The ladies in Vegas are hard to keep up with."

I let out a laugh, "You're already thinking about infidelity. You know how to make a girl feel special."

"I know how to make you feel a lot of things." Once again, his hand on my knee slid up my thigh, giving it a tight squeeze.

Squirming in my seat, I tried to get his hand off me, but he held a firm grip this time. "I think you made your point."

Looking around the place, I saw no familiar face. Gabe was making me uncomfortable. I had my hair pin-straight, but I felt the sweat on my head begin to undo it.

"Ms. DeCarlo," one of the hostesses approaches the table. "You have a call. Your cell phone is going to voicemail. Did you want to take it?"

Although odd, I took it as a chance to escape. "Yes, please."

As I follow her, she grabs my arm. "So that you know, if something like that happens again, be sure to order an angel shot. At least in here, it means you need help."

"Thank you," I reply, shocked. She picked up on how uncomfortable I was and decided to help. "So, no real phone call?"

"No," she smiled, "it was written all over your face you didn't want to be there."

Walking through the kitchen area, she led me to the back door. "Need a ride?"

"No, I drove."

"Hey, it's not my place, but you need to run away from guys like that. That's coming from someone who knows firsthand what domestic violence looks like."

I nod my head, "Thank you."

I was shaking from head to toe as I walked to my car. It felt as though I just escaped death. I can't do this. There shouldn't be anything the Appollo brothers have on my brother to make me go through with this. This ends tonight. Driving straight to Luca's lounge, I storm right in.

Everyone looked at me as I entered.

"Can I help you?" the bartender says as I walk to the bar.

"Luca. Where is he?"

The bartender laughs, "Wrong place, honey."

I laugh in return, sounding delirious. "Get me my brother. Now."

"Eddie, I got it." Emilio walks up from behind me. "This is Luca's sister, Bethany."

Eddie's face turned white with embarrassment. "My apologies."

"Don't worry about it." After Eddie walks away, Emilio turns to me. "What are you doing here?"

"I need to see Luca," I said.

"Shouldn't you be at dinner?"

"I'm not marrying that thing."

"That's not your call." Emilio pulls out a cigarette to light.

Pulling it right out of his mouth, "I'm making it my call. Emilio, that man is horrible."

"Did he put his hands on you?"

I looked away, not wanting even to discuss it. "Please."

After a pause, Emilio replied, "He's in the back. Go past the red door over there."

I storm through the red door, where I find Luca puffing a cigar on a sofa while flirting with a woman. I couldn't see her face as her auburn hair covered it as she leaned toward Luca, and they both laughed.

"Luca." I stood in front of them.

Turning his head to look at me. "Ah, B. You remember Veronica, don't you?"

"Bethany? Oh my god, it's been so long. You're all grown up!"

I realized who it was: Veronica Miller, one of Luca's childhood friends. She handles a lot of real estate in Arizona for my brother. I hadn't seen her in years.

"Hey," I tried to smile but wasn't here to be social.

"Veronica, why don't you go see where Emilio is."

Right as she left, I was going to dig right in, but Luca spoke first. Puffing on the cigar, "You will marry him."

"I had a hostess pull me from the table to save my ass. How can a stranger be more concerned about me than my brother?!"

"Emilio will speak to him."

It was clear that Luca wasn't going to budge.

"What is that going to do?"

"He will send a clear message," Luca replied.

"You think that will prevent him from beating me to a bloody pulp?!" I fall to my knees, "Luca, please. Don't let me go through with this."

"Why don't you get some rest? Tomorrow is a new day."

My brother didn't seem phased at all by my pleas. I get to my feet and leave with tears streaming down my face. As I drive home, I dial my mother.

"Bethany," she sounded as though she was sleeping.

"Hey, sorry to wake you."

"No, no. Is everything okay?"

"Luca wants me to marry an awful man, momma. Please talk to him," I begged.

I hear her pause and take a deep breath. "I'll see what I can do."

That wasn't a good enough answer. My mother's 'I'll see what I can do' says she will bring it up because she said she would not because it was a real concern. Did she want the same thing? Although siding with Luca wasn't out of the norm, I would have thought my plea for help on something life-changing would get her to speak up for me.

"Momma, please."

"I will talk to him."

Although it didn't sound reassuring, there was nothing else I could do about it. Pulling into the parking garage, I get out of my car and lock it. As I walk toward the door, I hear an extra set of footsteps behind me. Looking over my shoulder, I see a shadow. Picking up my pace, the footsteps behind me did the same.

I panicked, but I was so close to the door—just a few more steps.

"Ending the night without a kiss goodbye?" a voice echoed in the garage.

Turning around, I didn't see anyone. As I walk backward, I bump into a body. Instantly scared, I turned around and find Gabe looking furious. I couldn't even scream. My voice was lost. As he stepped toward me, I stepped back. He reached to grab me with one hand, and once he had a good grip on my arm, his other hand lifted over his head, ready to swing right into my face. Terrified was an understatement. Right as his hand was coming down, I closed my eyes. I've never been hit before, but I knew this would hurt. Ready for the impact, I brace myself. Suddenly, there was a loud sound, and I felt my face get wet. The grip on my arm loosened. Opening my eyes, I see blood spilling onto the floor and Gabe screaming. What was going on?

"Bethany! Go inside!"

Emilio pushes me toward the door. He had a gun in hand and was pointing it to Gabe's head. Gabe sat on the floor, holding his bloody hand. Everything felt as though it was going in slow motion.

"Bethany!" Emilio shouts. "Inside. Now."

I ran to the door inside the building but didn't go to my condo. Instead, I looked through the little glass window and watched as Emilio began to use the bottom of the gun to punch Gabe repeatedly. Emilio didn't hold back for a second; each hit harder than the last. Gabe was resilient and somehow managed to overthrow Emilio and throw a punch. Seeing them go at one another as blood from Gabe's hand-wound got everywhere. When I heard another gunshot and was unable to make out which one of them pulled the trigger, I turned and ran to my condo, locking myself inside. Looking in the mirror, I had above a console right when I walked in. I take a look at myself–there was a splatter of blood on my face. The red against my blonde hair popped.

What just happened? Suddenly, I had shortness of breath, and I fell onto the floor. Sobbing as I lay scrunched up in a ball, I felt helpless. Who knows how long I was there, but eventually, I managed to stop sobbing. There were footsteps outside my door, making me panic again. I could see the shadow of the person's feet while I lay on the floor as they stood there for a minute. Eventually, there was a knock, and I covered my mouth not to make a sound.

"It's me, Bethany."

Emilio's voice was soft, but I was still trembling from the incident just moments ago. I slowly got off the floor to open the door, and there he stood as though nothing had happened. This was Emilio. You never know where he comes from or what he does, but he always looks put together and is never stressed.

"Can I come in?" he asked.

I opened the door without an answer, inviting him in as I stepped back. Watching him watch me, I could tell he was uncomfortable, which was new. He shuts the door behind him in silence.

"You watched?"

"A little," I whispered in a shaky voice.

"He was going–"

"I know."

He didn't need to justify it—I was thankful. My eyes teared up. If he didn't show up, then who knows what Gabe would have done aside from beating me to a bloody pulp.

"Are you okay?" he asked, noticing I was shaking.

I nod my head but avoid eye contact.

Unexpectedly, he lifts me off my feet, carrying me to the shower. I remained silent. We didn't say a word as he undressed me and wiped the blood off my face. He took off his shoes and suit jacket. Under the jacket, he had on a gun holster that held a gun on each side. He rolled his sleeves and washed me while I stood in the shower. He was being so gentle with me, a completely different person than moments ago.

"Is he dead?" I whispered.

"No," Emilio replied. "Just needed a reminder of who he was dealing with." He winked at me.

After washing me down, he wraps me in a towel and takes me to bed. As Emilio pulls the covers over me, I grab his arm.

"Stay. Please."

Chapter 21

Movement on the bed caused me to open my eyes. Unlike the night before, we woke up cuddled up on each other. My naked body, still wrapped in the towel, clung to his side as my arm and leg draped across his body. He was still clothed in his shirt and pants. With one arm wrapped around my body and the other resting behind his head, I had peacefully slept the entire night. His movement woke me.

"Trying to sneak out?" I said with a sleepy smile.

"I need to get going." Emilio tried to pull his arm from under me, but I shifted my weight onto the leg draped over him so that I was now seated on his pelvis. "Bethany."

I ignored his warning and removed the towel wrapped around me. "I didn't get to thank you for last night."

Emilio locked eyes with me. "There's no need," he sat up, placing his hands on my hips.

"Yes there is."

He rolled me onto the bed so that he laid on top of me. "You should get some rest."

"I'd rather do something else."

Lingering over me, I could tell he wanted it but holding back. There was no reason to at this point. His face got closer to mine, and our lips were about to touch, but it all came to a halt when his phone rang. We both look at the nightstand and see Luca's name appear. I jumped off the bed to cover myself like he was in the room. Emilio reaches for the phone and answers. It was a quick 'yes' and 'will get there soon' before hanging up.

Just as he hung up, it was my phone that rang next. Now Luca was calling me. So, I answer.

"Where are you?" Luca asks.

"At home."

"I'm walking into your building now."

My nerves kicked up. "You're coming here?" I say out loud as I look at Emilio.

Without having to say much else, Emilio gathered his things quickly.

"You want to bring Mother into this. Then it's time the three of us have a chat."

"Mom is with you?"

"No, she is meeting me there."

And just like that, my doorbell rings. Emilio walked toward the window as though debating if he could jump out.

"I'm guessing that's her ringing the bell."

I quickly get off the phone and throw on a pair of sweatpants and a shirt.

"Just stay in here."

"I need to be across town," Emilio stated.

"Okay, I'll make sure we are in the living room. You can sneak out. That's your only option, or stay here until they leave."

Without much of a choice, Emilio nodded his head. I exit the bedroom and head for the front door to let my mother in. When I got to the door, Luca was standing behind her. Both of them had a serious look on their faces.

"Are you alone, dear?" my mother asked.

"Of course," I reply, watching to see if they are suspicious.

I let them in and take them into the living room. My mother sat on the sofa chair while Luca stood behind her, looking at me seriously.

It was silent for a minute before my mother started to speak. "Bethany, dear. I spoke to Luca about marrying Gabe Appollo. And we are at a standstill."

I scoff, "A standstill?" looking from one to the other. "The man showed up to my place last night ready to smash my face in for walking out on dinner!"

"Your brother has ensured that behavior will never happen again."

"Mother!" I shout in disbelief. "Luca has you wrapped around his finger. As always." I began pacing around the room. "I won't marry him. You can't make me."

My mother looked as though she pitied me, but not enough to change her mind.

Luca barely looked at me. "The wedding is in two days."

This threw me into a rage. "No!" I said, shaking my head as tears began streaming down my face. "I'll kill myself," I blurt out.

My mother looked down at the floor in defeat while Luca walked to the window, peering over the river.

With eyes full of tears, my mother looks up to me. "Bethany, dear. Have a seat."

I sat on the sofa closest to her. "Why are you making me do this?"

"The Appollo brothers somehow got a hold of information and intended to use it against us to fulfill a vendetta that we put behind us for the sake of our family."

A vendetta is a blood feud—a body for a body. Marco and his family were killed in vengeance for an act my father committed against the Cassariano Family. Normally, it's a never-ending feud until someone calls a truce or an entire bloodline disappears.

I roll my eyes. "How many times have people tried to blackmail us? It's never been an issue."

"This time, my dear, we are in a bind. Your brother doesn't have a way out without it causing a bigger problem for us."

"Father called a truce. The vendetta has been over."

Reaching out to take my hand, my mother begged me. "Please, Bethany. Trust us."

Pulling my hand away, I said, "That's all I've ever done. Look where it's got me. I'll never be truly happy, and it's because of him." My line of vision shot in Luca's direction. Speaking through my teeth, "Why do I need to suffer for the sake of this family?"

"Tell her." Luca's voice was stern as he continued to peer out the large window.

"Tell me what?" I asked, feeling a lump in my throat.

My mother cleared her throat. "You know family is important to me. It always has been. When your brother Marco passed, it killed me. Your father called a truce so that there was no further bloodshed."

"What does it have to do with this marriage?"

This time, Luca finally turned to face me, who answered, "Alfie."

"What about Alfie?" I was confused more than ever.

"That night Marco, his wife, and child were gunned down. We made them believe all three were dead."

My brain went blank trying to connect the dots through my rage.

My mother said, "Alfie is our last piece of Marco."

The room went silent. I got to my feet and turned away from them to process what I had just been told. Thinking back to that day, I remember running out of the house and seeing the horrific scene. Luca was holding a bloody and limp Marco. My father held my mother as she sobbed, trying to stand. My sisters checked Marco's wife in the passenger seat and baby

Paulo in the back seat. Rita looked to Luca and shook her head to let him know both were gone. Isabella rushed me back into the house and told me to stay in my room.

"I saw it with my own eyes."

"I noticed Paolo was lightly breathing," Luca replied, "I rushed him to the hospital. He lived, but I knew he couldn't stay with us."

Turning back around, "How could you keep that from me?"

"The only people who know are me, your father, and Luca. It was safest that way," my mother replied.

"So Alfie is really... Paolo? Marco's son? My nephew?"

"Shh," my mother whispered as though someone would hear.

"His name. He was in foster care. He followed Luca from California to Chicago." I was thinking out loud.

Luca placed his hands in his pockets, and the look on his face was full of emotion. He never let his guard down; it was a surprise to see. Or maybe he just wanted me to be sympathetic to the situation.

"B, we had to play it off." Luca breathed deeply, "He was five years old, and we needed him to forget us. I made sure he was put in a foster home with good people with nice monthly checks to cover all his living costs."

I laugh mockingly, "Of course. Why else would you take an orphan under your wing? It makes sense."

"Do you understand now?" my mother asked hopefully.

"I understand," I place my hands on my hips, "But it doesn't change my mind. You wanted me to partake in a plan I had no idea was going on."

"Bethany," Luca was done being emotional, "If it's known that he's alive, he will become a target."

"I don't care," I state.

"You should," Luca shot back, annoyed.

"You should have thought of that before having Aria here," I replied.

"Aria?" our mother questioned.

"Oh, you haven't heard?" I said maliciously. "Your son here is entering a Cassariano in this city, at his office and home."

The look of shock on her face was priceless, while my brother looked about ready to kill me.

"Luca," my mother was on her feet facing him, "Is this true?"

"Aria is working on the development project," Luca replied. "Bethany, don't try to deviate from the conversation."

"I'm not marrying anyone!"

Luca started walking off down the hall. "Go find yourself a dress. The wedding is in two days at the cathedral."

Chapter 22

"You can't change his mind?" I plead with Emilio. "You did it last time."

He shook his head and said, "I had good reason last time. Luca's mind is set on this."

Wiping the tears falling down my face, I knew why Luca was dead set on this, but I couldn't tell him.

"I will never forgive him for this."

Holding my chin up with the knuckle of his pointer finger, I said, "You should trust him. Whatever his reasoning, you should know he will ensure everything works out for the best by now."

"Not this time." I sniffled. "Who will come to save me when I'm all the way out in Nevada? Gabe isn't afraid to hit a woman."

A tear drops down my cheek, and Emilio wipes it away. "I can tell you one thing, sweetheart. You're not going to Nevada."

There was a glimmer of hope in my eyes, "I'm not?"

"I have a way to get Gabe to settle his roots in Chicago."

My body is slightly relaxed. "Thank you," I whisper.

"You can thank me another way." The look in his eyes told me what he was referring to, and I smiled in return.

I wanted to thank him, and not just because of getting Gabe to stay in Chicago; I wanted to thank him for always being there to save my ass.

"You're going to have to rip it off," I said, tugging on my shirt as I walked toward the bedroom.

Emilio smirked, "That won't be an issue." He removes his jacket and tie as he stalks toward me.

Lifting me, my legs naturally wrap around his waist, and he carries me to the bedroom and tosses me onto the bed. We locked eyes. The day was hot, so I wasn't wearing much, to begin with, but Emilio tore my t-shirt in half with his bare hands and then removed my shorts. Unclasping my bra, he throws it onto the floor; he hooks his finger into my lace thong, and I hear the fabric rip. The aggressiveness was turning me on. As I lay there naked, I watched Emilio undress himself. He was the kind of man that made you weak without even trying. His solid chest, perfect obliques, and v-cut were sculpted in perfection. With a hungry look in his eyes, Emilio was on top of me, sucking on my breasts while sliding two fingers in and out of me until I started to moan.

"Get on top," he demanded. As we switch positions, he looks at me, "Have fun, go for a ride."

Pleasantly surprised, I hover my entrance over his cock and slowly sit on it. Feeling him entering me, filling my insides, felt amazing. Fully seated and getting all of him deep inside me, I begin to move my hips forward and back. Starting slow and then picking up my pace, I could feel my body being possessed by him. Being the one in control felt exhilarating, but something was missing. Looking at him lying back with his head resting on the palms of his hands, he was letting me take the lead. Slightly lifting his hip a bit, his cock hit the spot inside of me, which caused me to yell out in pleasure. Picking up my pace, I could feel the orgasm building, but no matter how deep or fast I rocked my hips, I couldn't finish. On the other hand, Emilio seemed to be doing his best to hold himself together. My juices were running down Emilio's body and onto the sheets.

"Bethany, I'm struggling over here," he breathed through his teeth.

Panting, I reply, "I can't... I can't finish."

He lifted his hip again as though that would help, but it only strengthened the desire for release.

"Help me," I begged. Emilio was confused and looked concerned. "Tell me to cum."

A smirk crossed his face as he lifted his hip again and said the words I needed to hear. "Cum for me, sweetheart."

Just like that, my body obeyed his command, and my orgasm came bursting through. Both of us climaxing at the same time groans and screams ripping out of our mouths. I collapse on top of him, trying to catch my breath. My mind went blank as it had reset itself. Still delirious, I didn't even realize the words that slipped from my mouth.

"I love you."

Emilio said nothing; he just turned onto his side so that I fell beside him. He placed a kiss on my forehead and then got out of bed. I watched him get dressed. Was he leaving? Did I scare him off?

"I didn't mean it," I sat on the bed, holding the sheets over my chest.

"It's okay," he replies, putting his pants on. "It doesn't matter if you love me or not. You know the deal between you and I."

"Of course."

"Good." He throws on his shirt. "You have a big day tomorrow. Get some rest." Emilio walks out and leaves.

Chapter 23

The church bells rang right as I arrived at the cathedral. The sound was always calming to me, but today, it sounded as though it was my death sentence. Barely able to look at my brother, he walked me down the aisle in my designer fit and flare ivory gown with a modern straight neckline, subtle v-back, and a chapel-length train. The princess seams down the bodice were perfectly sown with inverted godets detailing on the sides of the skirt. I had wanted something simple but still feel bridal, so I softened the look by wrapping a delicate English net cape across my chest and around my shoulders, letting the rest of the fabric fall down my back. My hair was up in an elegant high bun with a crystal headpiece.

My mother in the front row pew was in tears. However, I wasn't sure if it was because her last child was getting married or if she allowed this to happen without a fight. She was the only one I could look at, even though I was mad with her just as much as I was with Luca. My sisters even tried to change Luca's mind but to no avail. My threat of taking my own life was a bluff Luca called. He knew I would never do that.

"I promise, B, I'll make it up to you," Luca whispered.

"Nothing you can do can compensate for this," I reply.

Finally reaching the altar, Luca handed me to Gabe. I force my eyes on him, wanting to smack the evil smile off his face. In return, I glance at his bandaged hand and shoot him an equal smile. He slightly twitched his mouth that sent a shiver down my spine. It took me back to the other night.

Luca may believe he set Gabe straight, but the look in Gabe's eyes told me otherwise.

Taking my hand, Gabe held it so tightly that I thought the blood flow would stop. Unable to get out of his hold, I dug my nails into his hand as hard as possible. He will need to know I won't be going down without a fight. As the priest spoke, we stood facing each other. When we got to our vows, I could see from my side view that his brother and family were smiling in victory.

"Do you, Gabriel, take Bethany as your lawfully wedded wife?"

"I do," he replied.

Now, it was my turn. "Do you, Bethany, take Gabriel as your lawfully wedded husband?"

There was a lump in my throat as I tried to get the word out of my mouth, but I was struggling.

"Yyess," I forced out.

The priest smiled, unknowingly, that this marriage was against my will. "I now pronounce you man and wife. You may kiss the bride."

I felt the vomit burning up my throat and then back down as I swallowed it. Gabe stepped forward and then disappeared from my line of vision. The sound didn't register at first, but as his head jerked to the side, blood splattered everywhere. I stood stunned as he fell to the ground. Screams filled and echoed throughout the cathedral. Something wet was dripping down my face. I looked down to see Gabe on the floor, his head busted open.

I heard my name as my brain tried to register what was happening. "Bethany!"

Next thing you know, I'm being hauled away to a private room. There, I find Luca and the rest of my family.

"What's going on?" I asked, shaking.

"I promised I would make it up to you," Luca said.

Right then, Emilio came walking through the door, quickly shutting it behind him. He hands Luca what appears to be a car lock keypad.

"They are all about to drive off now. Everyone is in place," Emilio said as he handed it over.

Luca takes the keypad and looks to me as he pushes the button. A loud explosion is heard. He presses another button, and another loud explosion occurs. Everyone in the room except Luca and Emilio crutched down onto their knees from the startling sounds that made the room shake.

Luca handed the keypad back to Emilio, saying, "Make sure to get everyone out of here individually."

Emilio nodded. As he walked out, he shot me a wink as I stood up straight. I was still stunned at what was going on. When the door was shut, there was a sigh of relief from my mother and sisters.

"Jesus, Luca," Rita said in a low voice. "Could you have made it any more dramatic?"

"I could have blown up the Church," he smirked.

My sisters and mother got to their feet.

As my mother fixed her dress, "Are you sure that is everyone?"

"That was everyone," Luca replied confidently, "They are put behind us."

"Aw, Bethany," Isabella came to my aid, pulling out a tissue and wiping my face that was saturated in blood.

Confused, I looked at the small mirror in the room. Looking like Carrie at prom, I stood there covered in blood from head to toe. The red blood stained my blonde hair, fair skin, and ivory dress like I was part of a freak show.

Three men walked in to escort my mother and sisters out of the cathedral. Turning around to face my brother, I was speechless.

"I told you I promise to make it up to you." Luca looked at me, trying to gauge what I was thinking.

Walking toward him, he braced himself as though I was going to hit him, but instead, I wrapped my arms around him. Squeezing him tightly.

Luca returned the gesture. "You think I'd leave my baby sister high and dry?" he kissed the top of my head.

"You could have done it before I had to say yes," I huffed.

"I'm a man of honor, B. The priest pronouncing you husband and wife upheld our end of the deal. What happens after that is off the table."

Pulling out of the hug, "Blowing them all up at once won't seem suspicious?"

"That was Emilio's touch on it. Alfie took care of the rest of them back in Nevada."

"Luca. Do you plan on ever telling Alfie about who he is?"

My brother shook his head, "He can't ever know B. Give me your word you won't say anything."

"Why can't he know?"

"Imagine growing up in a foster home with no one to adopt you and feeling unwanted and abandoned, only to learn later in life that you are the bloodline to the DeCarlo Family. The anger, hate, and loathing would turn him against us. I rather have him around as one of my men. Keep him close without having to worry whether he will resent us." Luca spoke as though he had the experience of going through something similar.

Emilio walked in, "Your car is out front. Everything is cleared."

Luca nodded to him, "Make sure she gets home okay."

Emilio and I were left in the room after Luca walked out.

"Married and widowed within three seconds," I comment, "That's a record."

Emilio walked toward me, "Are you okay? You've been through a lot the last few days."

"I think I'll manage." Holding my hands in front of me, "How do you do it?"

"Do what?"

"Look... calm. You just witnessed a man's head blown off and an entire family burst into flames."

He shrugged, "Just a regular day at the office."

His comment made me laugh nervously.

"Ugh. I look a mess." As though it would make a difference, I tug on my dress and smooth out my hair, trying to look put together.

"My dick's never been so hard. Go home. Shower. Put some sexy lingerie on. I'll meet you there once I get everything settled."

My dreadful day was making a turn for the better.

Chapter 24

I was still in shock by the events of the day. The image played in my mind of Gabe's head being busted open in front of me each time I closed my eyes sent shivers down my spine. None of the men there seemed to have flinched or found it as traumatizing. If something like that didn't faze Emilio, it made me wonder what did. The rumors of his torture must be true, but how can someone who has always been so kind to me be so cruel?

Walking into my bathroom barefoot, the cold ceramic tile floor kept me from replaying the gory image in my head. In the far corner, I had a hot tub that could easily fit four people. It was mostly there to give the bathroom a spa-like feel, but I've only used it twice. As I filled the hot tub with a cherry blossom scent bath bomb and warm water halfway, it was just enough to hit just under my boobs when I sat down in it. When Emilio calls, I tell him to let himself in and where to find me. Hearing him approach, I prop myself up in a seductive pose. When he finds me, a wicked smile crosses his face.

"Now that's a good way to be greeted."

He undresses as I watch him. This man had saved my ass countless times, and I hadn't looked at him in any other way than just as my brother's employee, but now, in front of me, he stood as my hero. Just not the typical hero. Instead of a cape, he wore a gun holster. With clothes on, he looked lethal, but as he undressed, I felt something I'd never felt before. Off came his shirt—his lean biceps covered in tattoos of various tribal elements and symbols. My eyes looked down his chest, tight abdomen to his v-cut as he removed his pants and briefs. Emilio joins me but rather sits next to me. He sits across from me with his arms propped on the edges. We just stare at each other for a moment. My hair was down, the ends submerged in the water. I wait for his command. I'm his for the taking.

"Make your way over here," he finally states.

I get to my feet so my full body is in view; seeing the spark in his eyes makes me bite my lower lip. Standing before him, he looks up, taking in the view. His hands are placed on my calves and glide up to my hips. Pulling me down onto his mouth, I grab his hair to help keep balance. The feel of his tongue inside me was intoxicating. He encouraged me to rock myself against him. The wet strands of hair pressed against my skin, and water dripped down my exposed body. The swirling of his tongue inside me made me grip his hair tighter. I began to breathe heavier, and after the first moan escaped my lips, Emilio pulled away. He pulls me down, spinning me around, making the water splash up. With eagerness, he grabs me by the pussy and guides his erection to my entrance. Once positioned, he pushed me down so that he was deep inside of me. The pressure as his cock charged through me had me gasp as I reached behind me to the edges of the jacuzzi. Emilio wasted no time gyrating my hips against him—his fingers digging into my sides with a ferocious grip. Water splashed everywhere. I was on the edge of an orgasm.

"Don't you fucking dare!" Emilio's voice was husky and stern. "You don't cum until I fucking say so."

Unable to even speak words, I nod my head. But that wasn't good enough; he wanted a verbal answer.

"Bethany," he growled through his teeth, "Do you understand?"

I mumbled something.

Taking one hand, he wraps it around my neck. "Bethany!" he continued to move my hips aggressively. "Do you fucking understand!"

I muster any strength I have and let out a shout, "Yes! Yes! I fucking understand!"

Unsure I could last, I do a kegel squeeze that sends him into his frenzy. The grip around my neck tightens.

"Bethany," he warns.

Knowing I could take control gave me satisfaction, so I continued to do it until Emilio got frustrated and threw me off of him. Falling into the water face first, Emilio got up and turned me onto my back, so I floated. Getting on his knees, he opens my legs and rams right back inside of me. Pounding inside me even harder as I tried to stay afloat, I didn't know how there was still water in here. Practically drowning, I flop my arms to keep from going under. The sound of water splashing onto the walls and the floor was like a wild fantasy come true.

"Not yet, Bethany."

Emilio pulls out of me and slams back inside over and over, causing my eyes to roll behind my head. I was devouring every moment. Once his thumb made its way to my clit, I knew we were almost there. Part of me was relieved to finally orgasm, while part of me wanted this to last forever. Lightly circling his thumb over my clit, my moaning got louder as the build-up of my orgasms picked up its pace.

"Nipples."

Following directions, I grab my nipples. Emilio pushes himself as deep as possible inside me, furiously pulsing. There was no way I was able to last much longer.

As he applied a hard press on my clit, he finally said, "Now."

We both exploded, and I saw stars as his semen filled me. I was barely phased that I could drown. Pulling myself up and sit, I lean back waiting for my body to recoup. After catching our breath, we left the hot tub, dried ourselves off, and went to bed. Emilio extends his arm for me to lay beside him. My body is pressed up against his side, and his arm is wrapped around me as he lies on his back, looking up at the ceiling.

"Told you I'd get Gabe to settle in Chicago."

I nudge him.

"Too soon?"

I scoff, "Way too soon."

"Were you scared?" he asked, still looking at the ceiling.

"Kind of. Was it worth it? Going through all of that?"

Emilio looked down at me, "To save you from marrying that scumbag? Yes."

"Do you honestly enjoy what you do?"

Looking back up to the ceiling, "Depends on the day."

I rest my head on his chest. "How about today?"

"Today was a good day."

"So you like the gory stuff?"

"It's not about that. Sometimes, things are done for the better—that's when it's not so bad. Like today, 20 people are dead. But it freed an innocent person from life with a sleazeball. Your brother took a crazy gamble with you."

"He had reason to."

"Do you think it was worth it?"

Emilio didn't know the truth about Alfie, so I wasn't sure how to answer.

"Luca has a way of having his cake and eating it, too. He always has."

"You should have taken that job in L.A. after college."

Surprised he'd remember that, I lifted my head and placed my chin on his chest so I could look at him. "Wasn't part of the deal. I was able to go to college out of state but then I was to return to Chicago."

"Do you regret that?"

"I used to. But honestly, if I hadn't gone, I'd be stuck in Chicago forever." I place my head back on his chest. "Why did you guys leave California?"

"Our job there was done. It was time to come home."

"Can I ask you something? And I don't mean to offend you. I'm just curious."

Emilio laughed, "Go for it."

"How did you get the scar over your eyebrow?" The more I looked at it, the more I wanted to run my tongue along the mark.

Emilio smirked as he looked up to the ceiling while the event must have played through his mind again. "I was being accused of something I didn't do. The made men of Chicago back then handed me over to a NY family like I was leftover trash. I meant shit to them. I could have been killed that night, but I wasn't. I had my first encounter with a Consigliere face-to-face. Seeing the respect they got and the power without the responsibility of being the boss changed my perspective. He may have given me this scar, but it became more than that. It was the turning point when I decided I needed more in life than what I had."

"Why did he let you go free?"

He glances down at me, "Because of you."

Chapter 25

He glances down at me, "Because of you."

"Me?" I questioned in surprise.

Emilio nodded his face, and his eyes went back up to the ceiling. "The night of the incident I was being accused of was the night I first saw you."

I couldn't remember what he was referring to. The only memory of meeting Emilio was when Luca brought him around.

Sensing my lack of memory, "You were barely a teen. You and your friends stole Skittles or something stupid from the bodega."

I laugh, "My god, I forgot about that."

"You better pay for that!" the cashier yelled as we tried to leave the store.

"Put it on our tab!" Tiffany yelled as we dashed out.

"If I go to jail, my parents will KILL me," Natasha freaked out.

We thought we were badasses for stealing candy from the little bodega. As we ran, the cashier came out and started yelling at us.

"Damn, kids!"

Laughing, we turned the corner, and a few men were hanging around a car. We slowed to a walk and giggled until the cashier made his way around the corner and started yelling at us.

"Hey, Hey. Bernie, Relax," one of the men said, calming the cashier down. He spoke to the cashier, and whatever was said made the cashier return inside.

The man turned to us as we stood there like deer in headlights. "What are you girls doing?"

"None of your business," Tiffany spat out.

The man overlooks her and makes eye contact with me. "You're Marco's little sister."

I nod my head.

"Sorry for your loss. Marco was a good guy."

Swallowing hard at the thought of my older brother, whom we buried just a few weeks ago, I mutter, "Thank you."

"E!" a piercing voice screeched. A petite blonde approaches us, "Is that the little DeCarlo? Ask her about Gio. Maybe she knows something." She sounded worried.

He looked at her; they had similar facial characteristics. "Cass, relax." He turned back to me. "Hey, if you could ask Luca to give Emilio a call. It's important. He'll know who I am."

"Sure." I wasn't sure if I should trust him. What if he told Luca I was stealing? I wouldn't hear the end of it.

Sensing my concern, he assured me, "I won't rat you out but don't pull that shit again. Next time, Bernie will pull out his gun, and he never misses his target."

"Thanks," I tremble.

"That was before you worked with Luca. You didn't have to do that."

"I'd like to think someone would have done the same for Maria. That's how it works on the streets."

"Maria?" I question.

"Youngest sister," Emilio replied in a low voice.

"You had another sister? I didn't know that."

It seemed like he needed a moment of silence. Something must have happened to her, and asking seemed that it would open an old wound. So, I left it at that.

After a minute, I asked, "How did you get Luca to appoint you as his right-hand man?"

"I earned his attention saving your ass. I kept it by having the balls to carry out any request he wanted." He laughs, "At one point, he went wild just to see how far I'd go."

"Clearly, you surpassed his expectations. Luca was always particular with who he surrounded himself with."

"We had a mutual goal. Plus, I wanted to make sure Cassie was taken care of."

"She looks the type to be able to handle herself."

"It's a security thing. Not everyone grew up as privileged as you. Cass and I needed to hustle so that we could survive. It's been me and her for so long. She's all the blood I have left."

"She doesn't come around much."

"Cass never really liked the idea of me becoming a made-man. She has her reasons. So, she doesn't come around unless it's just her and I."

"So you don't see her often?"

"We have dinner three times a week. We speak on the phone every day."

"I didn't know you were close."

"If anyone knows my darkest secrets, it's her."

Tracing my finger on his chest, I said, "I wish Luca and I were that close again. He's not the same person."

"That's not a bad thing, Bethany. He evolved because he needed to, but that doesn't mean he stopped caring."

Deep down, I knew that, but I couldn't separate the man he was from the man I knew him to be now.

"Well, with the Aria in the picture now. That's all he cares about."

"Jealous, Bethany?"

I roll my eyes. "Can I confess a secret?"

"If you trust me enough to keep it."

"I never wanted to be anyone more than I want to be Aria. She's bold and fierce. She's stunningly beautiful, and her confidence matches Luca."

"That comes with age. Don't think Aria had it easy."

"I know, I know. She left the lifestyle and made it on her own. But at the end of the day, she is still who she is. And we are no more than five years apart. She just has it all together."

"A lot can happen in five years."

In my mind, I knew a lot could happen in a much shorter time frame. It was no more than two months ago that I was aching for something, and little did I know it was someone like Emilio.

Chapter 26

"Get him fitted for a pair of shoes."

Anyone outside the lifestyle wouldn't know what that meant. Cement shoes were a mobster signature move. It wasn't something you'd read about in the paper. Made men don't gloat about their art of getting rid of people—at least not the smart ones. There was no chance unless someone ratted you out and no one dared to rat on Emilio. I've heard the rumors; Alfie is even terrified of him. He'd never speak of it, but I knew he witnessed how far Emilio would go to punish those who crossed the DeCarlo Family.

Aria was in town; she alternated her weeks between Chicago and California. How she managed to handle the travel and excessive work was impressive. When Luca was busy entertaining Aria, Emilio gave me his attention. I gave myself to him willingly in any way he wanted.

Wearing a sheer see-through mini cami dress with thin straps, Emilio had me positioned on his marble dining room table on display to his liking. I remained on my knees, spread apart with my hands held behind my back, waiting for him to return from the call that disrupted our session.

Walking back into the room, Emilio was fully dressed in a black suit carrying a small black satin pouch. "Are you okay to stay here for a bit? I need to step out."

"Okay," I was disappointed, but asking me to stay meant he would return soon to continue this.

"I want to come back to you begging for it." Standing at the end of the table, he demands, "Come to me."

placing on my hands on the table, I crawl to him. When I reach where he is, I sit up straight onto my bare ass. Emilio ripped the sheer fabric off my body and tossed it to the side while we never break eye contact. He reaches into the pouch he placed on the table and pulls out a pair of handcuffs. Taking the cuffs, he locks them around my ankles—the metal was cold and sent a shiver through me. They were snug against my skin and kept my legs from moving apart. Next, Emilio pulls out the rope and ties my hands together before me, leaving one end out.

"Really," I asked. "This is how you want me to beg for you?" Looks more like I'm being held hostage.

He ignored my comment and hopped onto the table, holding the pouch in hand. Taking the loose end of the rope, he drags me back to the center of the table. His shoes sounding against the table echoed in the room. Without saying a word, I let him continue. I trusted him. Emilio ties the loose end of the rope to the crystal chandelier hanging from the ceiling. Looking up at him as he stood on the table looking down at me, he opened the pouch to pull out a long chain. I was confused when I saw the chain had four ends with clamps attached.

My eyes widened; I wasn't sure if I was nervous or excited. With a smirk, Emilio pushes my hair behind my shoulders, then takes two clamps and attaches one to each nipple. I suck in air as I adjust to the pressure. Emilio got down on his knee, grabbing the other two clamps, and I gulped as I waited to see where they would go. Using two fingers, Emilio separates the lips of my pussy, causing me to gasp as the air hits my clit; after waiting a few seconds and watching my reaction, he places one clamp on each labia. Immediately, a moan escaped my mouth, and I was lightly panting.

"I'll be back soon, sweetheart." Emilio places a kiss on my forehead and then tugs on the chain.

"Oh fuck," I reply, breathless for words.

Sliding off the table, Emilio looks at me and shoots me a wink before leaving. He wasn't kidding when he said he wanted to find me begging for it. I don't think I can last; my body was reacting, and if my hands were free, I'd be handling things myself.

I don't know how long I was there, but when I heard the door open, I propped myself up in a desirable position. The sound of shoes on the floor getting closer was stimulating my body to prepare for what was to come. I needed Emilio inside me immediately. But instead of Emilio, who enters the room, it is his sister Cassie.

"Ugh," she huffed, shaking her head, "I knew my brother was doing something stupid, but I didn't think this stupid."

Embarrassed, I tried to scrunch my body as though that would help hide anything. Cassie jumps onto the table and begins to untie the rope from the chandelier; my arms collapse beside me.

Cassie was mumbling to herself the entire time, "The DeCarlo sister. Of course. Pick the most off-limits person he could."

Without shame, Cassie removes the clamps gently from my nipples and then labia. I was ashamed that my arms were too numb to remove them myself.

"It wasn't him," I replied. "I made him."

Cassie didn't want to hear any excuse, "That doesn't make the situation any better. Not that you would care what happens to him."

"I do."

"If you did, honey, then you wouldn't be naked on his table, all tied up." She looks at my ankles. Then, she looks around the table until she sees the black satin pouch. Pulling a key out, she uncuffs my ankles.

"He wasn't supposed to tell anyone," I comment.

"My brother keeps his word," Cassie replied without looking at me. "All he said was to come untie someone at his place because he would be awhile. So he didn't tell me a thing." I give her a look, and she scoffs. "Don't worry, honey, I'm not saying a word. I don't want my brother to die over some broad."

Trying not to sound insulted, "I'm not some broad."

I always thought broad described a street girl or a classless lady.

"To me, you're some broad. Unfortunately, you're also a DeCarlo."

"Your brother is Consigliere. That's an honor." I swing my legs off the table and get onto my feet.

"Yes. But fucking your boss's sister is not." Cassie walks out of the room, returns with a blanket, and tosses it to me. "God forbid anyone finds out and tells Luca, one of us will be losing a brother."

"Luca wouldn't hurt Emilio." I wrap myself in the blanket.

"You sound so sure of it," Cassie spit out. "Emilio is all I have left. And if anyone takes him away from me, they will pay for it."

I thought she was ready to rip my head off. She walks off again, leaving me behind. Cassie scared me. She was a wild beauty, almost the male version of Emilio. I never interacted with her directly; she didn't care about faking nice. To me, she was intimidating. Cassie wasn't the kind of girl to fall in line because she was told to.

Walking into Emilio's room, I get dressed and grab my things. When I walked out, Cassie was still there drinking gin straight. Next to the bottle of gin was wine and a glass.

Cassie nodded her head to the wine, "Want a drink?"

Surprised by her sudden change of mood, I took it as an opportunity to get to know her, but she seemed to have an agenda of her own.

"What's the deal with this Aria?" she asked as I sat.

I pour myself some wine and reply, "What exactly do you want to know?"

"She's banging your brother, right?"

I laugh, "That's a question you need to ask him directly."

"She gets around," Cassie said as she downed another shot. "She is good-looking, though; I can see why my husband is attracted to her."

I remembered what Emilio had said: she was married to the guy who faked his death and became the Consigliere to the Cassariano Family.

"You're still married to him?" I questioned.

"Well, I thought I was a widow for years until we found out he was alive. My brother said Gio be done for if he stepped foot in Chicago."

"Wasn't he here recently?"

Cassie gave me the side eye, "Thanks to that bitch."

"But Emilio hasn't..."

She knew what I was implying, "Like I said. Thanks to that bitch. You know how it is—they shoot you with 'It's part of the plan' or 'We have a deal.' Blah blah blah."

I was all too familiar with that. "How did you find out he was alive?"

Cassie downed a shot, "Another story for another day."

We sat there drinking and just talking about life. Things we wish we did and things we wished we didn't. Chances we should have taken and ones that were taken from us. She dove into her childhood, and I didn't realize how rough they had it. One thing we had in common was how we both lost a sibling.

"Emilio was the one to find her. She was in the bathtub," Cassie recalls choking up. "She was a kid. Emilio always blamed himself. He was a street kid and thinks she wouldn't have done it if he were home more."

It was a heartbreaking story. In my opinion, it's worse than Marco's death. Being in the lifestyle, there's the chance you won't live, but to find someone who took their own life wasn't just heartbreaking but a devastating shock.

"How did your parents take it?"

Cassie poured another shot, "What parents? We don't even know if the three of us have the same father. Our mom was a junkie in and out of rehab. She dropped dead last year; cheers to that."

We hear the door open, and Emilio appears to find us drunk on his sofa.

"I see you both are having fun," Emilio walks over and takes Cassie's almost empty bottle of gin.

"You like them young now, huh?" Cassie spits out with a smirk.

Emilio sucked his teeth. "I told you to come in, do what I said, and then leave."

Cassie laughed, "Kinda hard to leave when I see who's tied up."

Getting to my feet, I said, "I'm going to use the restroom before I go."

I stumbled a bit, but Emilio caught me in time before I fell. "I'm taking both of you home."

I managed to get myself to the bathroom and back in one piece but stopped in the hallway when I heard Emilio and Cassie speaking. They whispered but it echoed through the room, and they must've not realized I would be able to hear them. Standing in the hallway, I listened.

"You're a sucker for chicks with big tits," Cassie said.

"Relax, Cass. It's just sex."

"Does she know that?"

"Of course."

"Girls like her get attached. If you break her heart, you're screwed. End it. Now."

I remained silent the entire car ride, playing on being drunk. My head leaned onto the window as I watched the buildings pass by. Emilio drove up the private ramp to reach the parking garage on my floor. He parked and exited the car to open the door for me. The summer heat entered the AC-filled car.

Helping me out of the car, I force a smile, "You don't need to walk me to my door."

"A gentleman always walks a lady to her door."

It was a nice gesture, even though Cassie's words buzzed in my head. Did people think I was that fragile-minded? A ball of emotion was stuck in my throat. I knew this was just sex, and I knew one day it would end, but the thought that it would happen sooner than expected was making me sad.

"You're a quiet drunk," Emilio said as we walked down the hall.

"Just not feeling well," I replied, forcing another smile. We reach my door, and I turn to face him. "Thanks for the ride."

"I'll have your car parked in your spot before you need it for tomorrow." Emilio pulls me in and places a kiss on my forehead. His lips were plump, and the softness against my skin felt soothing. "Goodnight, Bethany."

He waited until I let myself in. As I shut the door, I lean against it, my head tilted upward. Shit. I was that girl. When did it happen? Like a rug pulled out from under me, nothing was there to break my fall. The end was coming. I could feel it, and I wasn't ready.

Chapter 27

Aria was due to leave for New York tomorrow, so I planned to make tonight one that Emilio would thoroughly enjoy. I began dreading when Aria would leave Chicago, knowing Emilio would no longer come around. He was adamant about keeping his distance when she wasn't distracting Luca.

While shopping for some new lingerie, Emilio calls me.

"Lucky you, I'm at your favorite store," I answer.

"Tonight isn't going to happen."

"What? Why?"

"Aria is leaving earlier than planned. Your brother and I have a little meeting at Chaos tonight."

"Okay," I replied. "You can't just come later?"

"Don't hold your breath."

We got off the phone, and I couldn't help but be disappointed. Tossing what I had in hand back onto the rack, I walked out and did some retail therapy instead. This month flew by, and I hadn't realized how attached I had become to Emilio. He's all I thought about, and I got butterflies anytime he came into sight. My phone rang again; this time, it was Alfie. Sometimes, I wished that I didn't know the truth about him. I didn't know how to act and somehow, I couldn't remember how I treated him beforehand.

"Hey, Alfie," I answer.

"B, I'm back."

"Back in Chicago?"

"For the weekend. Can't miss Tiffany's party."

The fourth of July was around the corner, and Tiffany was throwing her yearly epic bash on a rooftop hotel for a pool party. It was always full of Chicago's finest men and women.

"What plans do you have tonight?"

"Meeting Emilio and some chick at Chaos tonight."

My stomach dropped. Emilio said he was meeting Luca.

"What chick?" I asked.

"Some blonde. She comes to Chicago from time to time."

My blood boiled while I was getting off the phone. I felt like a fool, but I won't be made one. I texted Natasha and Tiffany that we were having a girl's night.

ele

The place was packed out as we made our way through the crowd. The girls danced as we walked to the bar while I kept my eyes open to see whether I could spot Emilio. The club was hot, and even though I was dressed in a cropped pink tank top and matching shirt, my body was sweating. After a round of shots, I shouted to them over the music that I was going to the restroom. Leaving them, I head toward the private room area; he had to be there, but nothing. The only other place was the showroom. Although she looked familiar, I couldn't place my finger on who she was.

Unlike last time, the two guards let me in without a fuss. Walking in, the room was fuller than last time. Scanning the place, I see Alfie seated on a chair, speaking to a woman I've never seen before. She was blonde, and I wondered if it was the one Emilio was meeting up with. As I got closer, I could make out the features of her face. Her blue eyes sparkled, her blonde hair tied into a bun, and I thought her red lipstick made her look cheap.

"Having fun?" I asked as I joined them.

Alfie was surprised to see me. "B, how'd you get in here?"

"I'm a DeCarlo, remember?" Part of me felt guilty rubbing it in his face, knowing the truth. I need to remind myself to hold back those kinds of comments. "Who's this?"

The blonde looked up at me, sizing me up. I'd never gotten into a fistfight before, and I was sure if that happened right now, she would win. Any woman dressed in leather pants in June was ready to brawl at anytime.

"Grace," she smiled, extending her hand.

"Bethany," I returned the gesture.

She turns back to Alfie, "Kid, where the hell is Emilio? I don't have all night."

"He should be around here; I'll check the bar."

He left us there, and to me, it felt awkward, but Grace leaned back in her chair and swung one long leg over the other. Her pant leg rose a bit, and I saw a butterfly tattoo. She screamed badass—something that would catch Emilio's attention for sure. I couldn't help but feel jealous and insecure. Unlike Grace, I was the typical rich brat in Emilio's eyes.

"So you're Luca's sister?"

"That's right," I smile.

"Aria's mentioned you."

"Me?" I was surprised.

"She's mentioned you've been making her feel welcome here."

I smiled but felt guilty; my kindness was just a ploy to get her to trust me and use whatever she may say or do against her. That's the only reason Luca wanted me to start a friendship.

"Chicago is a tough city; having a friend on your side is good."

"I heard she met your mother briefly," Grace was laughing. "I wish I was a fly on that wall."

Again, I felt guilty for that, too. My mother wasn't happy with Aria being here and staying with Luca, which she wouldn't have known if I didn't open my mouth.

"You must be good friends with Aria if she told you that."

"We grew up together."

Why would Grace, who is close to Aria, be in Chicago meeting Emilio? Surprised by the information, I asked, "So, how do you know Emilio?"

"Just happened to be at the right place at the right time and saved my life. I'll never forget that."

"He's a good guy under all that darkness."

She gave me a look that said she wasn't so sure. Maybe she's seen that side of him often enough to forget there was any kind of goodness.

"He has a soft spot for damsels in distress."

I laugh, "You don't look like a damsel in distress."

"Younger Grace was. Times have changed."

"Grace," Emilio appeared and greeted her by shaking her hand. "Bethany, what are you doing here?"

I was so eager to spy on him that I didn't think it through that if he saw me what I would say—so I had to think of something on the spot.

"Natasha and Tiffany wanted a girl's night. Alfie said he was coming here and figured I'd say hi." I got to my feet.

There's no way Grace was a threat if Emilio shook her hand. I excused myself to return to the bar to enjoy the rest of my night. Alfie stood there speaking to one of the guards at the door.

"What was that about?" he asked me as I approached him.

"What?" I asked innocently.

"You popping in like that?"

"I can't come say hi?"

Alfie gave me a suspicious look. "Luca send you?"

"No... why would you think that?"

"To check on me."

I got nervous. "Why would he want me to check on you?"

"It's been weird lately around here."

"Weird, how?"

Alfie shrugged with one shoulder. "Luca called me back when I was supposed to stay in California for a while. Emilio's been... nicer. I was surprised he was trying to get me to stay in Chicago since he was so eager to get rid of me."

"You're overthinking it," I replied. "What's Grace's deal?"

"She comes to the city every once in a while."

"You think they are sleeping together?"

"E and Grace?" Alfie thought about it. "Doubt it. E doesn't mix business and pleasure."

I trusted Alfie's instinct, so I sighed a breath of relief. Leaving the showroom, I got back to the girls who were now on the dance floor.

"Where were you?" Natasha asked.

"Saw Alfie and was just catching up."

As the night went on, we drank and danced. This time, I behaved myself, unlike the time on the dance floor. In the distance, I see Alfie walking Grace out. A smile crossed my face as it confirmed that Emilio wasn't having a thing with her. Liquor was flowing through my body, and I was feeling promiscuous. I sent Emilio a text asking if he was here but didn't get a response.

At the end of our favorite song, I shout to the girls, "I'll be back."

When I went to the door of the showroom, there were no guards, and the door was locked. I guess it was done being used for the night. If I were Emilio, where would I be? I scanned the club but didn't see him. Walking toward the private room, I asked familiar faces if they had seen him, but they didn't. The private room was empty, which was disappointing. Maybe he left. I checked my phone, but he still hadn't replied. A waitress happens to walk in to grab something from the bar.

"Hey, have you seen Emilio?" I asked.

"Should be in the office."

Hmm, that should be fun. As I head toward the office, I push my boobs together, making sure they looked perky. Getting closer to the door, I could see the light on from under the door. I knocked before opening it, only to find it was empty. What was going on? Stepping out of the office, I walk further down the hallway. There was a strange sound that got louder the more I walked. It was a clapping sound. Turning a corner, I see a woman with her legs around a man's waist as she was pinned against the wall. Each time the man thrust forward, it created a clapping sound followed by a thud from her body getting hit against the wall. They were still dressed; the woman just hiked up her skirt, and the man unbuttoned his pants. Standing there, I couldn't take my eyes off them. Hearing him grunt, he pulled out once he was finished. I sigh in relief when the man turns around, and it isn't Emilio.

Giving up on searching for him, I return to my friends. We were there until the place shut down. As I got to my car, I finally got a text back from Emilio.

> **Emilio P.**
>
> Home. Everything okay?
>
> Was hoping to catch you before you left ;)
>
> Busy night. Tomorrow, I'm all yours.

Although I wasn't as drunk as I was earlier, the alcohol was still very much influencing me, and I knew better than to drive, but my body was aching for him. I didn't want to wait until tomorrow. I reach his building safely and stumble to his door with my heels in hand. Putting my shoes back on so that I could pose for him when he opens the door, I fall back onto my butt with a loud thump.

"Shit," I spit out as I held my ankle, which was throbbing.

The door opened before I could move to get back on my feet. Emilio stood shirtless, his sweatpants hanging off his hips. The sight took my breath away and a smile was beginning to cross my face until I hear a woman's voice right before exiting the door.

"I'll keep you posted."

When she came to full view, I saw it was Grace. She looked down at me with a confused face. Her red lipstick was completely off, and her hair, which had initially been up in a bun, was now undone, falling past her shoulders. So much for feeling secure with her and Emilio. Then it hit me. She was the woman I was watching at the last sex party and I've seen her around Chicago before that as well.

"Bethany?" she asked.

Embarrassed, angry, and ashamed, I was speechless. My vision was getting blurry as they began to water.

Emilio cut in, "Get back safely."

Grace hopped over me and left while Emilio glared down at me.

"What are you doing here?"

I shrug because if I were to speak, I'd begin to sob. If I were able to run off, I would, but the shooting pain in my ankle was getting stronger. Emilio huffed as he bent down to grab me to lift me into his arms. Shutting the door behind him, he takes me to the kitchen, placing me on the island across from the fridge. He pulled out cubes of ice and placed them into a cloth so that he could ice my ankle.

"You shouldn't have come here," he stated without looking at me, pushing his hair back with his hand.

"Why, so that I wouldn't be insulted knowing that you are sleeping with other people?"

He held the ice around my ankle a bit tighter. "Bethany."

Pulling my ankle away from him, "Emilio."

Not letting go of my ankle, he pulls it back toward him. "What do you want from me?" he steps closer so that his other hand is leaning on the countertop beside where I was sitting. "If you think this is going somewhere, you need a reality check." He leaned in closer to my face. "This is what I didn't want to happen. I knew you'd get attached."

All I could muster was, "Get off of me."

His words cut deeper than they should have. He was right—we weren't dating or ever discussed exclusively sleeping together. I didn't mean to get attached. Now I sat here looking and feeling a fool. All I wanted to do was end the night and forget this happened.

Emilio stepped back, letting go of my ankle and handing me the ice. Taking it, I avoided eye contact. I hopped off the counter, landed on my good foot, and limped.

"Where are you going?" he asked.

"Home. Where else?" my reply was sharp.

He lifted me over his shoulder and headed to the bedroom without warning.

"Please put me down," my skirt rode up, and I could feel my butt cheeks were exposed.

"You can't drive. Stay the night, and I'll get you a ride in the morning."

Walking into his bedroom, he removes the covers and flops me onto the bed. Rather than lay beside me, he leaves. He shut the door as he left the bedroom, leaving me in the dark. My heart felt heavy as I turned onto my side and cried myself to sleep.

As I opened my eyes, they were puffy. I forgot where I was for a second until taking a deep breath into the pillow, and the scent of eucalyptus and mint reminded me. It almost had me crying again. Rolling off the bed, my ankle was doing a lot better, and I could walk on it for the most part. One of the dressers had a mirror over it, and I took in my appearance. Looking a mess, I try to fix myself up best. My purse was in the kitchen, and I had no idea what time it was or if Emilio was awake. He never came into the room last night.

Slowly and quietly, I open the door and tip-toe down the hall. The lights were all out except in the bathroom, where the sound of the showerhead ran. I breathed a sigh of relief that I could sneak out without seeing Emilio. Making my way to the kitchen, I pick up my heels, scattered on the floor with my purse and phone, then dash to the door, exiting quietly. I've never driven home so fast, skipping the 4th of July holiday traffic before it got out of hand.

Walking through my front door, I toss off my shoes and head for the shower. The plan was to take a nap before Tiffany's pool party. I was going to need the energy to get through. Fresh out of the shower, I went to grab a bottle of water when my phone pinged from receiving a message. Grabbing it, I was confused by the name on the screen. Giovanni Pancelli. Why did that name sound familiar? Why was he calling me? Or maybe the question was, how did his number get saved onto my phone?

Entering the passcode, the phone wouldn't unlock. Getting annoyed, I begin to examine the phone. The back had one of those wallet inserts, and I pulled out the driver's license to see that it wasn't my phone. It was Emilio's. Confused, I looked into my purse and saw my phone was there. I had several missed calls from Alfie. A smirk crossed my face. Emilio must be in hysterics, needing his phone returned, and since he can't contact me directly, he would need to be discreet. It felt like I somehow had the upper hand and wouldn't disappoint.

If Emilio wants his phone, he will need to get it himself... but first, I was going to have some fun with it. Tiffany's parties were full of attractive men, and I plan to use it to my advantage. These butterflies for Emilio need to die and fast. I'm catching feels for a man who just has me on his roster—another notch on his belt to wear out.

Emilio can't be the only one to have all the fun, and I wanted him to know it.

Chapter 28

It was hot and the perfect day to have a pool party. Tiffany outdid herself this year, and the guest list was pretty big, with even bigger guests. Natasha and I scan the deck for any potential hotties to hit on. My baby pink rhinestone bikini left little to the imagination. With my hair tied up so my body was in full view at every angle, I was on a mission and wasn't leaving until I was successful.

"Let's grab a drink and head toward the pool."

We walk toward two lounge chairs reserved just for us—perks of being good friends with the host. Tiffany would be running around greeting and mingling with all the guests before she could enjoy her party, so we let her be. Lounging while sipping our drinks, Natasha and I people-watch through our dark sunglasses.

"There are a lot of important people here," Natasha commented.

"Chicago's elite," I replied. "I guess her party has become a summer highlight."

Daughters and sons of the city's wealthiest families scattered throughout the rooftop, leaving their prim and proper manners at the door. It was Las Vegas brought to Chicago.

"See that guy by the other end of the pool? Brown hair and American flag trunks with the sunglasses that match his trunks?" Natasha pointed out.

Checking him out, I reply, "He's cute."

He was of average build, with blonde hair and skin tanned by the sun. He would have blended into the crowd if it weren't for his patriotic swim trunks.

"He's the D.A.'s son."

"I didn't know the D.A. had a son."

"He recently graduated from Dartmouth Law School," Natasha replied.

"How do you know all this?"

"He entered the bar one night like some big shot. So I had to know the scoop. He came in with four girls, and they told me all about him. He's going to follow in Daddy's footsteps. How cute, right?" she laughed.

I roll my eyes. "These elite girlies are going to be all over that."

Natasha nudged me, "Maybe... but it looks like he has his eyes set on someone in particular right now."

I roll my eyes as I catch him looking at me. He shoots me a wink. "Politicians aren't my thing."

"Well, he isn't one yet."

"Legal authority," I nod in his direction, "DeCarlo," I point to myself.

"Point taken." Natasha laughed. "Looks like he's headed our way."

"Ladies," he smiles.

Thankfully, my shades covered the annoyance in my eyes. "Hi."

"I'm Hamilton."

I did my best not to laugh; he even had a preppy name. "Hi, Hamilton. I'm Bethany, and this is Natasha."

"Let me get you ladies a refill."

"Only if you promise to get lost afterward."

My response took him aback. "Do you know who I am?"

"No," I replied. "But you should know who I am."

He smirked, "If you were anyone important, I'd know."

I hit back. "Everyone in this city knows the name DeCarlo."

He lifted his shades over his head. "You're a DeCarlo?"

"I am."

The side of his mouth curved up just a little. "You're the kind of trouble I like."

"You're not my type," I smile.

"You'll question that if you get to know me."

"You sound confident."

"And you sound interested." Putting his shades back on, he said, "I'll be back with drinks."

As he walked away, Natasha giggled. "Do you need to be mean to EVERY man that hits on you?"

"It wouldn't be me if I wasn't," I shrug.

Chapter 29

Hamilton brought us over a round of drinks and was charming as ever despite me not reciprocating. As he spoke, I didn't even bother making eye contact with him as I scanned the crowd. The sight of a girl wearing red lipstick sparked an internal rage within me, reminding me of my mission. Why keep looking for a boy toy when there's one right in front of me? Turning to Hamilton, I gave him my full undivided attention.

"I knew a good drink would change your attitude."

"Or maybe it's just your lucky day," I reply.

Hamilton and I were heavily flirting for some time, giving me the impression that he wanted the same thing I did.

"I'm going to scout for Tiffany," Natasha excused herself. "It's no fun being the third wheel."

She got up and left. Hamilton and I looked at one another—without saying another word, we mutually agreed on what we wanted to do next. With a smile, Hamilton grabbed my hand and led me out of the party. We entered the elevator, and I watched him hit one of the floors. Interesting, he was staying here tonight. I guess when you're looking to get laid, it's easier to have a room ready at hand.

Once inside the suite, he offered me a drink. As he prepared it, I pulled out Emilio's phone and placed it on the console behind the sofa. I didn't know the passcode, but I could still use the camera feature. I put it on video mode and propped the phone against a vase discreetly so Hamilton wouldn't notice.

"Gin and tonic for the lady," Hamilton smiled sweetly.

We both knew what we came for, and there was no need to delay it. Taking the drink, I place it on the coffee table, then push him down onto the sofa and have him watch me strip tease. Slowing untying the back of my bikini top, I seductively pose for him so he would take in the sight of me before removing my bikini bottom. He leans forward, taking my leg and placing my foot on the sofa beside him. His hands glide up my thighs as his head moves closer to my opening. Right went his hands reach my bare ass, he pulls me in, and my body quivers at the feel of his tongue entering between my lips.

I place my hand on his head, putting a firm hold on it as I move my hips against his face. His tongue dove deeper inside me, and I was relishing every moment. I began moaning as his tongue moved feverishly inside of me. He pulled away while pulling me onto him, and our mouths collided. Needing to ensure this was all caught on video, I put my weight onto him as I remained straddling him. As I moved my hips slowly, rubbing against him, I could feel him getting completely stiff.

He extended his arm to a box on the coffee table that held condoms. As he put one on, I kissed his neck and winked at the camera phone. Once the condom was fully on, I lifted my hips and sat on his cock. He slid in easily, and I took a moment to adjust before I started to move my hips up and down gradually while he sat back and enjoyed. Letting Hamilton watch my body move as I put on a show, my hands fall down my face to my neck, then over my breasts slowly and stopped at my navel.

My eyesight went to the phone, and a light smile crossed my face as it was strategically placed in the perfect position, exposing me in full view. Placing one hand on Hamilton's bare chest, I glide the other down to my clit and begin to touch myself as I start to pick up the pace leaning slightly back so that my phone catches the entire view. Hamilton was panting, and he muffled it by shoving one of my breasts in his mouth. The tension in all my weak places started building. Beginning to moan, I was being louder than I normally am. Just thinking about my voice ringing in Emilio's ear turned me on.

Forgetting completely about satisfying Hamilton, it caught me by surprise when he pushed me back onto the coffee table in front of him and got onto his knees, thrusting into me as he pushed my legs over my head. Emilio had me in this position plenty of times, so I had to make it sound like I was enjoying it more with Hamilton. Although he was not bad, I couldn't stop thinking of Emilio. Anytime I closed my eyes, his face popped into my mind, so I kept them open and focused on Hamilton and the phone.

Hamilton came and held onto my legs as he caught his breath. He noticed I hadn't orgasmed, so when he pulled out, his fingers went inside me, making a particular motion that instantly sent me over the edge, but what I didn't expect was for me to squirt all over his chest. I screamed in pleasure as Hamilton's chest got soaked. My body tensed while feeling the multiple orgasms overtake me. I lay limp on the table as a happy Hamilton looked down at me.

"That was good," I commented.

Hamilton smiled, "We should do this more often."

"Anytime you want it."

I get off the table as he lifts his trunks back up. Quickly reaching for the phone, I hit stop on the record button. It was automatically saved to his phone, and I couldn't hold back the evil smile. I wanted Emilio to know how easily he could be forgotten.

"Let's head back to the party?" Hamilton suggests. "My friends are probably looking for me."

"Sure," I reply as I reach for my bottoms. "I need to head out anyway. Can't miss the show."

"What show?" he asked curiously.

"Every year, my brother hires pyrotechnicians to put on a firework show while we take one of our boats out onto the river to watch."

"I've heard of it. It's Chicago's highlight."

"That it is. I'm sure you'll be able to see it from the rooftop."

"Or I can come with you."

Surprised by his eagerness, "Why?"

"Meeting Luca DeCarlo is a big deal."

"Mhmm," I place my hand on my hip.

"Fucking his sister is another," Hamilton shot a smile to redeem himself.

"Unfortunately, it's family only."

He crossed his arms against his bare chest, not believing me. "Embarrassed of me?"

"No," I walk over to him, "But if you come, then he will think we are dating, and let's just say not many people have been able to handle Luca."

"I'm not 'many people,'" he shrugged, "I'm a stand-up guy. I can play along."

I laugh, turning him around, "Let's get back to the party."

"You can introduce me as your boyfriend."

Raising my brows, "You don't want to open that can of worms."

"Look, my father wants me to marry one of these Stepford wives' type of chicks. But if I tell him you and I are hanging out, it will get him off my back. I'm sure you don't have that issue, but being the son of a powerful politician – who I am with is a big deal."

I did know how it felt, but I wasn't going to get into that. Maybe it wouldn't be so bad, and it'll kill a few birds with one stone. Luca would be impressed; my mother and sisters would get off my back, and Emilio would see how it felt dangling someone else in front of him.

"Go put on a shirt. We have a boat to catch."

Chapter 30

Feeling satisfied as we returned to the party, I found Natasha and Tiffany to say my goodbyes.

"Where have you been?" Natasha asked.

"With Hamilton," I smirk.

"You got with Hamilton Branton?!" Tiffany squealed. "Kathy Harrington is going to die. You know how much she hates you!"

It made me laugh. "Well, I just gave her another reason to."

I spot Alfie in the crowd, "B! Where have you been?"

"Mingling," I replied.

"Let's go before we miss the boat."

"Okay, I'm ready." Hamilton joined us.

"Who the hell is this?" Alfie asked.

"Alfie this is Hamilton Branton. Hamilton, this is Alfie Pelton. He's like a little brother to me."

They shake hands.

"Let's get out of here," Alfie replied. "Emilio has been on my ass today."

"Really?" I asked. "How so?"

"He's in a pissy mood. He's using his backup phone. Apparently, his cracked."

I smirk, "That sucks."

The night air was a lot cooler, and there was a breeze. Hamilton gave me one of his hoodies, which I wore with shorts over my bikini. We arrived at the river, where a boat was waiting for us to board. My family was there waiting for me to carry out this yearly tradition. Walking onto the boat, I instantly saw Emilio, which made my insides tingle. Alfie was not joking when he said Emilio was in a mood. It was written all over his face, and his jaw clenched when we made eye contact. He knew this had to be a discreet conversation so he couldn't approach me. But when a woman wrapped her arms around him, it felt like he had a one-up on me again.

"I'm underdressed," Hamilton whispered.

An instant relief came over me. Two can play this game, and I had Hamilton to flaunt.

"So am I," I smile, looking down at myself wearing shorts and a hoodie over my bikini.

"Who is this?" Luca's voice took our attention.

I introduced Luca to Hamilton, and they shook hands.

"Why are you here?" Luca directly asked Hamilton.

"Bethany invited me, and I wanted to meet the family."

Luca looked at me confused, "I didn't know you were dating someone."

I shrug, "It's new."

A breeze shifted the scent of mint and eucalyptus in my direction. Within seconds, Emilio stood with us.

"Bethany," Emilio addressed me.

"Emilio," I smile, "Who is this?" I asked, referring to the woman.

"Rachel," she smiled.

Alfie and Hamilton began talking about sports, which made me lose attention. My mother and sisters came over and gushed over my date while I couldn't help but watch Emilio and Rachel off to the side, flirting. He had his arm around her and whispered into her ear, making her giggle. I could vomit right here. What tipped me over the edge was when she went in for a kiss. Those were my lips not hers.

My brother's voice beside me pulled me out of the thought of clawing Rachel's face.

"Is everyone ready for the show?"

We all sat in the open area lined with chairs and watched the fireworks explode above us.

As the night sky lit up in colors, I rested my head on Hamilton's shoulder. My plan of having Hamilton here worked well for everyone except Emilio, who didn't even seem to notice. I got up to get a drink at the bar—every event, no matter how small, always had alcohol.

"Gin and tonic."

The bartender handed me the drink.

"Let me get a Macallan."

The sound of Emilio's voice made my heart beat faster.

"Bethany," he said my name, but I refused to look his way.

"Emilio," I replied, sipping my drink.

"My phone."

Slyly, I pull it out of my bag and place it on the bar. "Here you go."

He took it and walked away without any further interaction. If having Hamilton here didn't phase him, my video wouldn't either. Feeling stupid, I take my drink and sit back down. He was playing along with this whole thing well. Toward the show's end, I go to the lower deck to use the restroom.

I hear whispering.

"The feds raided the house. They took Lorenzo in. Trust me, they have much more to focus on," Emilio said.

"Is Aria still coming?," Luca asked.

"She will be encouraged to. Grace gave me her word."

My brother worries a lot about Aria and what is happening with her. I continued to walk to the bathroom. When I got out, it was quiet. Suddenly, I was pushed into one of the rooms, and the door was quickly shut.

Emilio stood in front of me, looking very angry. "You have some balls, sweetheart."

"What are you talking about?"

"That video you have on my phone." He spoke through his teeth.

I had practically forgotten for a moment, but seeing him agitated like this put a smirk on my face. "Did you like it?"

This seemed to upset him more. "What are you trying to pull here, Bethany?"

Continuing to act nonchalantly, "Nothing."

Stepping toward me, he didn't stop until I was pushed up against the wall. His dark brown eyes seemed darker. He wasn't even touching me, but having him this close had my brain malfunctioning. I knew I didn't have the same effect on him, and it killed me. I hated that he was so unphased by my presence that the only way I knew how to get a reaction was to get under his skin.

The fireworks outside continued to burst into the sky, casting different colors into the room through the small window. Emilio's chest went up and down as though trying to control his anger, while mine was due to our tension.

"Why." It was more of a demand than a question.

"It was an accident," I replied.

We were locked into a dead stare-off.

"You accidentally had some other man inside you while filming it?"

The reference took me back; I thought this was about taking his phone.

"Oh, that was on purpose." I purposefully tilted my head with an evil grin.

Emilio clenched his jaw, but rather than come off scary, he was coming off sexy. His dirty blonde hair, perfectly styled, made me want to run my hands through it and mess it up.

"Didn't I tell you no one else should see what I do?"

"I don't think Hamilton got the memo."

His hand grabs my neck unexpectedly, which makes me inhale sharply. My entire family was on the deck just a steps away.

"If you aren't going to fill him in, I'll do it for you."

Chapter 31

I roll my eyes and call his bluff. "In front of everyone?"

He leaned his head so close to mine that my heart started rapidly beating out of my chest. His lips brush against my ear. My cheeks started burning, and my body shivered from fear and anticipation.

"No one will question it." His breath against my skin had me melting.

"My brother will."

Although I couldn't see his face, I could feel the sadistic smile on his face. "Not if I show him the video."

The sudden feeling of fear was rooted in the pit of my stomach. If Luca even saw that video, he'd have Hamilton hung by the balls off a tree.

"You wouldn't." I pushed him off, but his hand remained on my neck.

"I would, and you know it."

"So you're going to use this against me now? That's pretty low for you."

"That was your mistake, sweetheart." Emilio loosened his grip around my neck. "You shouldn't try to one-up someone who is always a step ahead."

I felt his words, not just heard them. He was going to teach me a lesson, and I knew I wasn't going to like it.

"Stand right here and watch," he demanded.

Remaining where I was, Emilio opened the door to let someone into the room. What was he doing? Rachel, the woman he came with, enters but is unaware I am there. He positioned her so she wouldn't be able to tell I was standing in the corner. There were no words exchanged between them, just eye contact. I watch as she removes her shirt in one swift move—her breasts pop out, and instead of wearing a bra, she has on nipple clamps—one on each nipple with a chain that is connected to each end. The chain discreetly hid under her low-cut shirt perfectly. Emilio, in the meantime, had unbuckled and pulled down his pants.

He yanks on the chain to pull her closer to him. As he kissed and bit her neck, his eyes were on me. This wasn't a lesson. This was payback, and I was getting a front-row seat. This was beyond insulting. The look in Emilio's eyes told me to stay in my place, leaving me paralyzed as I stood there in shock.

Watching him lift her skirt over her hips, she seductively called his name, "Emilio."

This prompted him to lift her, in which she wrapped her legs around his waist and arms around his neck. I could see his cock enter inside of her, and she whelped from the friction as they jumped right into it, although that didn't stop them from continuing. Emilio lowered her onto him until he was fully inside of her. Tightly holding her thighs, he pumped in and out of her so aggressively that the chain from the nipple clamps jingled all out of tune. The sound of her cries of pleasure would have been heard throughout the boat if the fireworks weren't being fired. Never for a second did he stop looking at me. I ruptured with jealousy.

"Ahh, Emilio!" she screamed when he tossed her onto the bed.

As he continued to thrust in and out of her, his hand went for the chain. He pulled, causing the clamps to stretch out the nipples. Rachel grabbed the sheets, her eyes rolling back as she basked in pleasure. The harder he pulled on the chain, the louder she yelled. Pulling out of her, he spills his semen all over her breasts right at the firework finale.

It wasn't fair. Emilio was allowed to sleep around, but I couldn't? All I did was send a video, which he could have deleted without having to watch the whole thing. I felt like a little girl who got scolded. Embarrassed and disgusted, I dashed out of the room and to the bathroom to throw some cold water onto my face. When I looked in the mirror, my eyeliner ran down my face. Heartbroken from a man that isn't even mine was starting to drive me crazy. I felt my mind losing its sanity. Since when did anyone disrespect me like this and get away with it? I am Bethany DeCarlo. Maybe it's time he knew what I was capable of. If this is how he wants to play—then so be it.

Mark my words.

CHAPTER 32

EMILIO

Was it crossing the line? Sure. But this is who I am. If you think you can mess with me, then you have another thing coming for you. My blood boiled when I saw the video. What was Bethany thinking? Despite the distasteful act, the real issue is why the hell it bothered me so much. Never in all these years did I inappropriately look at Bethany—after all, I met her when she was just ten years old. When did it all change?

"Was she here the whole time?" Rachel asked, embarrassed as she wiped my cum off her chest with the cover on the bed.

"She walked in and then ran out," I lied.

Using Rachel to teach Bethany a lesson was a low blow, I know. I wanted Bethany to feel the pang of pain and then some after I watched only a few seconds of the video. I could almost forgive her for filming that video on my phone. I knew why she did it. When she appeared at my place last night, right when Grace left, the heartbreak was written all over her face. She cried most of the time after putting her into my bed; I only knew that because I sat listening at the door on the other side the entire night. Part of me wanted to console her and tell her it wasn't what it looked like. Grace didn't come over to hook up; she was getting something done for me.

But it was better that Bethany had a taste of reality. I knew she was catching feelings. Things were getting too serious, and she needed to understand that I couldn't offer more than what this was. And our fling couldn't be anything more than just that.

"*Luca!*" *the sound of Bethany's voice filled the foyer. "I'm back!"*

She returned as a new college graduate. Being gone for four years didn't seem like much, but when she came into view, I couldn't believe my eyes. She walked wearing a short yellow summer dress and wedges, her hair freshly done and looking completely different from the last time I saw her. Then she was a child, and now before me stood a beautiful woman.

"*He will be back soon,*" *I said. "Congratulations on graduating."*

"*Thanks, Emilio,*" *she smiled. "I'll go hang out with Antonio until he gets back."*

Watching her walk away, I had to shake the naughty images in my mind. Then I notice Alfie standing beside me.

"*Stop drooling!*" *I smack Alfie behind the head.*

"*Who is that?*" *he asked, staring.*

"*Bethany. The youngest DeCarlo,*" *I replied. "Do I need to say she's off limits, or do you want to learn the hard way?"*

"*She's hot.*" *Alfie flinched when I raised my hand to him, "But I won't touch! Promise."*

"*Good.*"

As the last firework was shot, we joined everyone back on the boat's deck. Everyone was enjoying the show. Scanning the deck, I noticed Bethany and that preppy douche off to the side talking. She was flirting with him, and he was loving it. I found myself in front of them, and with a smile, I pushed the jerkoff over the railing and watched him fall into the water.

"Emilio!" Bethany shouted in disbelief.

"You think I was joking, sweetheart?"

I could tell she was pissed, but the sound of the jerkoff splashing into the water and Bethany's reaction caused others to approach us.

"What's going on?" Luca questioned.

"He just tossed Hamilton overboard!"

Everyone looks into the water to see the jerkoff whaling his arms and legs to stay afloat. Alfie throws him a life vest.

"What did he do?" Luca asked me.

I look to Bethany who was even more pissed off. She hated how her brother would disregard her.

"He made some wise-ass remark," I replied.

He turns to Bethany, "I guess he needs to get accustomed to how we do things around here."

I loved when she rolled her eyes. Watching the emerald-colored eyes disappear and trace back again did something to me.

Turning to me, Luca nodded for me to follow. As we walked to the other side of the secluded boat, Luca leaned on the railing, looking out into the water. For some reason, the river gave him a sense of peace and clarity.

"This can be good," Luca said. "Bethany and the Branton kid."

"The kid's an idiot," I replied. "Casper was better."

Luca laughed, "You're the one who found out he was sexualizing her around Chicago, but now he's better than this kid?"

"I also told you Gabe Appollo was a bad trade. You still don't trust my gut?"

"Gabe was different. I had to. And I know you're upset about not being in the know, but trust me, it's better that way."

I didn't argue or hold a grudge anymore over it. That night at the club, when he agreed to the terms of the Appollo brothers without my two cents, he insulted me. Maybe that's why I gave in to Bethany's advances. The morning Bethany was told who Alfie was, I just happened to be sneaking out at the exact same time and overheard it. I understood why Luca felt the need to keep it a secret but to know he didn't trust me with it pinched a nerve.

In private, Luca didn't mind being more casual when we spoke to each other. Part of him wants to think we can be friends. After all, men like him don't have any. They can't. Part of me believes we are friends even though being his Consigliere will always come first. I respected Luca for several reasons. He clawed his way to the top without caring about anything or anyone. But he wasn't able to get there without me. We were a team, and we held respect for each other and a lasting loyalty. Because of that, it killed me that I wanted Bethany, knowing each time I thought of her naked was an insult to Luca as a friend and as my boss.

"You never told me who pulled the trigger on him."

I smirk, "And you never will."

Luca didn't know it was Giovanni Pancelli, from the Cassariano Family, who did it for several reasons. In this lifestyle, if someone gets in trouble with law enforcement and is put on the stand during trial, the less you know, the better. You can't lie if you don't know the truth. Luca would be livid if he found out who did the deed, but I knew he'd never push to find out. Giovanni owed me for convincing Luca to keep Aria in Chicago. I used that favor to save Bethany from the disastrous choice of a wedding. There was no regret in helping Bethany but it wasn't like me to use a favor like that to help someone else.

"Have you heard from the blonde?" Luca asked. "How is Aria taking the raid?"

I furrowed my brows, "As any female would, but she's hanging in there."

"She is coming back?"

"I don't think she should. You know she will be watched like a hawk. We don't need law enforcement on us."

We were secure in our city and had a few federal connections, but not enough to make me feel good about housing a Cassariano under watch.

"I don't care," Luca replied, "Get her here and find a way to keep her here."

I huffed, "Give it to me straight, Luca. You have feelings for her?"

He didn't have to say a word; I read it in his eyes when he turned to look at me. I simply nodded in acknowledgment. Great. Now I have something else to worry about.

How the hell is a Cassariano and a DeCarlo going to make it work?

Chapter 33

"So, tell us what happened when you left with Hamilton?" Natasha wanted all the details during our lunch date.

"He came to watch fireworks, got tossed off the boat, then drove him home," I shrugged my shoulder. "He hasn't stopped calling me since."

Tiffany laughed, "Should I ask why he was tossed off the boat? Did your brother have another fit?"

I blushed. Unable to tell them the real reason, I just went along with what they just assumed.

"You know how Luca gets," I smile as I look at my freshly painted nails. Pink really never went out of style for me.

Even though Emilio pushed him off the boat, Hamilton loved every moment. To be in the presence of Luca DeCarlo or any of his associates was the biggest flex aside from being the D.A.'s son.

"Okay, so he wants to see you again after that?" Natasha chimed in, "That's a good sign!"

"Tash is right, B. I'm even impressed if Hamilton survived the first time meeting your brother and still wants to come around."

I take a deep breath, "You're both right. Maybe he's worth looking into."

But I didn't want to look into Hamilton or anyone else. That would mean ending things with Emilio, and the thought of that upset me.

"Just one date," Natasha encouraged.

Rolling my eyes, "Maybe."

"Bethany," I could sense Hamilton was smiling on the other end of the phone. "Finally, get a call back. I was starting to think the number you gave me was a prankster leading me on with text messages."

"Sorry, I just have a lot going on."

"Let me take you out," Hamilton said. "Please don't let me beg."

I huff into the phone, "Fine. Tonight."

"I'll pick you up at 8 pm. Text me your address."

Hamilton was prompt and was knocking on my door at exactly 8 pm. Opening the door, I find him dressed in a light grey suit, white shirt with nice dress shoes. The scent of expensive cologne lingered around him, giving him a more sophisticated demeanor.

"You smell nice," I comment.

"Thank you. And you look gorgeous," Hamilton smiled.

Wearing a cream-colored satin wide-legged jumpsuit with thin straps crossed in the back, I enter the hall. Holding a thin jacket in one hand and a clutch in the other, Hamilton couldn't hold my hand, so instead, he wrapped his arm around mine. It put a slight smile on my face; no one had ever done that before.

"Are you practicing walking down the aisle?" I teased.

Hamilton blushed, "Girls usually like some kind of physical holding. I was trying to be a gentleman."

We walked to his car, and he opened the passenger door to his Mercedes-Ben E 450 Cabriolet. It had a white exterior and black leather interior. Sitting in the passenger seat, I couldn't help but notice it smelled like the car freshener black ice.

"So where are you wining and dining me?" I ask as he drives off.

"One of my favorite restaurants just outside Chicago."

"Outside Chicago?"

"The best seafood restaurant, hands down."

I was getting nervous about leaving Chicago. I needed to let my brother know, but I didn't want to sound like a child who needed to call her parents for permission.

"Can't wait," I smile.

Just outside Chicago shouldn't be bad, right? We arrived at the restaurant and were seated in a private dining area. The waitstaff was on top of everything, and the food was impeccable. To my surprise, the conversation flowed nicely; we had more in common than we thought.

"Doing theatre was one of the worst things my father forced me to do," Hamilton recalls, "One year, my school put on a play of the opera Donizetti's Lucia di Lammermoor. Somehow, I got cast as a lead when I barely did an impressionable audition, which I was late for."

I laugh at the thought. "You managed to play basketball, be on the debate team, and play theatre? Impressive."

"I think it was to keep me out of trouble."

"Did it?" I asked.

"Hell no. Being a Branton, you kind of get to slide through life. I fully took advantage of that."

We may be from different worlds, but our uptight upbringing was similar. "I got to give it to you, Hamilton. Not bad. I may have to come back to this restaurant without you."

"Wow, using me for my good tastes?" Hamilton joked.

"Can I get you the dessert menu?" the waiter asked.

Hamilton shot me a look, the same one from the pool party.

"I think we'll grab dessert at home," I reply.

We barely reached my front door before we were on each other. Taking off our clothes as we made our way to the bedroom. I collapse onto the bed, pulling him down with me as our mouths never separate from one another. Hamilton's tongue rubbed against mine as our mouth-to-mouth contact intensified by the minute.

"Shit," he pulled away, "Let me get a condom."

Hamilton rushes to grab one and slides it on as I touch myself so I'm ready to receive him. He seemed excited watching me do so. When ready, I sit up on the bed and slide my hands around his ass and pull him forward so that he's standing between my legs. Placing my lips onto his abdomen for a quick kiss, I slowly get to my feet, licking him to his neck until our mouths meet again. We fall onto the bed with Hamilton on top of me.

His hands at my waist slide up and over my breasts while I wrap my legs around him. Placing one of his hands onto the bed for support while the other positioned his erection at my entrance. Slowly and gently, he enters inside of me, and I moan in response. His strides were deep, and he kept a steady pace.

"Harder," I encouraged.

Hamilton began thrusting with a bit more strength, but I needed more.

"Harder," I said again.

And so he did, but it still wasn't enough. I think he was being gentle for a reason. Maybe he wanted to uphold his good-boy image, but I knew the truth about him. He was a wild boy, and I wanted him to show it to me.

"Fuck me like you'll never see me again."

"Bethany –"

"Shut up and fuck me."

Hamilton nodded. Getting onto his knees, he held my legs wide open as far as they could go and began to ram his hips forward repeatedly with solid force. His momentum and stamina were staggering. When he saw how much I loved every hard, forceful hit, he held my legs tighter and opened them wider, enjoying the moment just as I was. Then he pulls a fast one on me as he throws my legs to the side and lifts me onto my hands and knees while still inside me. Hamilton grabbed my hips and rammed into me, yanking me back to meet his thrusts. Burying my face in the sheets, I scream in pleasure. Harder and harder he goes, sending me into a wild orgasm. After a few more pumps, his body goes rigid, and his grip tightens as he finishes. We both go limp onto the bed and are completely knocked out.

By the time Hamilton woke up, I was showered and dressed, having coffee in the kitchen.

"No breakfast in bed?" he joked, buttoning his shirt.

I smile, "I'm not much of a cook."

"When can we do this again?"

"Soon?," I shrug.

"I didn't make a good impression?" he asked.

"I didn't say that."

"So what are you saying?"

"I'm not saying anything."

Squinting his eyes, "You don't trust me."

"I don't know how to trust anyone."

Walking over to me, he kissed my cheek. "Learn to trust your instincts. Then see what it has to say about me and follow that."

Chapter 34

There was a strange feeling floating around the office. Most people were either on a job site or working in their office. The only ones buzzing around the office were Aria's team. Even her business partner, Nate, came into town to visit. All the female admins here in the office kept checking Nate out. He was very attractive—black hair and blue eyes. You could tell he wasn't from Chicago; he looked too delicate compared to the men here. I found it amusing that the women here drooled over Nate while the females on Aria's team from California would turn into mush whenever Luca was around. And I've caught several of them sliding their phone numbers onto Emilio's desk.

I was at the receptionist's desk, speaking to the new hire. Administration new hires were always entertaining because they were eager to make a good impression—as though that would catch Luca's attention. Working here was a big deal, even if your job was just answering phones and booking appointments.

"Anything juicy going on today?" I asked Susie—a high schooler working the summer while our original receptionist was on maternity leave.

"No. Pretty quiet for the most part." She always wore a smile, something no one around here did. "How was your 4th of July?"

"Pretty mellow," I internally laugh to myself. "Yours?"

"Spent it with my boyfriend. Making the most of the summer before it ends. We were going to different colleges and decided to go our separate ways."

"You both planned the breakup?"

Susie shrugged, "If we are meant to be, we will find our way back to each other."

I nod my head, "Very mature approach."

The elevator door opens, and in steps, a man with a large bouquet of yellow roses is placed on top of a rolling cart due to its weight.

"Wow, someone is loved," Susie commented, getting on her feet to prepare to receive the package.

"I bet it's for Aria," I joke, "Notorious for getting an overwhelming delivery of flowers."

The man approaches the front desk. "Delivery for a Bethany Ann DeCarlo."

My jaw dropped open. Susie looked at me with a smile. "Guess Aria has some competition."

Walking over to the bouquet, I pull out a card that reads:

I loved dinner, but dessert was better. I hope to do it again.
From, Hamilton Branton

I couldn't help but smile. No one has ever sent me flowers after a first date or even bought me this large of an arrangement before.

After signing for the package, I looked to Susie and said, "Have one of the assistants bring this to my office."

"Sure, Bethany," she smiled.

As I walk away, I call Hamilton.

"Someone is a show-off," I comment, laughing when he answers.

"Good thing I didn't go for the larger option."

"There's a larger option?" I walk into my office. "I've never gotten yellow roses before. It's different."

"I took a culture class in college. In some cultures, it shows admiration."

"Hm, if that's true, that's sweet. If it's not, that's a smooth line."

Hamilton laughs. "I had a good time last night."

"Me, too," I admit.

As I look up, I see Emilio passing by. I managed to avoid him all morning. I hadn't seen him or my brother for the rest of the weekend. The longer I can avoid him, the better. I was still annoyed with how he handled the boat ride. It was going smoothly until the end of the day. As I was getting ready to leave, I was stopped by Molly.

"Hey, Emilio said he wanted to see you in his office."

I smile uncomfortably, "Thanks."

As I walked into his office, I saw Aria still working. These glass walls sometimes were so invasive. Not that Aria would question me being in his office, but it felt like she would be part of this conversation. Opening the glass door, I find Emilio seated on the sofa in the center of the room.

"You wanted to see me?"

Emilio was reading the paper and didn't look up, "Are you going to ignore me now?"

I scoff, "Trust me, if I could never see you again, then I would. Ignoring you is the next best thing."

Emilio looks up and tosses the paper to the side. "You know that's not possible."

"Is that what you wanted to tell me?"

"I'm not sure why you're upset with me."

"Really? Did you forget what happened the other day?"

"Which part?" he challenged. "When you took my phone? Or when you filmed yourself? Or was it when you took my phone to film yourself so I could see it?"

I roll my eyes. "More like the part you fucked another girl in front of me."

"Sounds like you like to give the jabs but can't handle taking them."

I shifted on my feet. "You started it."

"I don't remember starting anything."

"Ah, so you forgot about the blonde from New York?" I didn't even want to say her name.

"She's a friend."

"Yeah, just like Rachel is, right?" I cross my arms against my chest.

"No," Emilio replied, "Rachel and I have a past."

"So you have no boundaries on who you sleep with."

Emilio smirked, "My boundaries don't need to be to your liking. You don't see me complaining about the prick who sent you flowers."

I roll my eyes, "It's a friend."

Emilio raised his brows, "That's hypocritical of you. Bitch to me about no boundaries, yet you are doing the same."

"I'm not doing anything," my hands went to my hip. "You don't know what you're talking about."

"Just like I don't know how you went out of Chicago for dinner?"

"Have you been stalking me?"

"Your brother doesn't give me much of a choice."

Frustrated with the conversation, "Why did you need to see me?"

"Aria's brother was arrested and will be charged a few things. Luca wants Aria to feel welcomed."

"She's already very welcomed here. What more does he want?" Her presence here was starting to become irritating.

"What if it was Luca, Bethany? How would you take it?"

He had a point. If Luca were arrested, I'd be a mess. "Fine. Is that all?"

"No."

"What else do you need?"

"I think you know the answer to that." The devilish look in his eyes pulled me in.

"Right here?"

"Your mouth wrapped around my cock, right here."

Surprised at the bold comment he'd made in the office, I looked next door to Aria, who was getting ready to leave. But what was more confusing was why I was willing to do it.

My mouth went dry. "What if Luca shows up."

"He's at home waiting for Aria." Emilio reaches for the phone on the console at the end of the sofa and speaks into it. "Susie, turn the lights off when you leave." He hangs up the phone.

"Feeling adventurous today?" It was surprising he would want this done in the office.

"Feeling something," he replied.

A knock on the wall startled me. It was Aria's leaving and waving goodbye. When the lights in the front of the office turned off, we knew no one else was there. He sat on the sofa, waiting for me to do my thing. It was thrilling, something I have felt with him since we've started this whole arrangement. I wanted to stand my ground but I couldn't and he knew it.

I removed my blouse slowly, followed by my bra. The air brushed against my skin, causing my nipples to harden. He loved my tits, so I made sure to push them out for his viewing. Slowly, I walked toward him as he pulled out his penis and began stroking it as he watched me. As I dropped in front of him between his legs onto my knees, Emilio grabbed my breasts, each hand holding one while his thumbs rubbed my nipples, making them even harder. As I stroked his penis, he would rub and twist my nipples with more pressure. Once fully erected, he leaned back so I could do my thing. I was on a high and feeling proud, taking it all in without a gag. Slurping and sucking, twirling my tongue around his shaft, I went all in, grabbing his balls to massage them. Saliva dripped from my mouth, and I moaned so that he could feel a vibration. Emilio was trying his best to hold out for as long as possible, but once I shoved his cock deep down into my throat, all hope was lost. His semen shot down my throat, and he let out a moan of satisfaction. Once finished, I lifted my head with a big smile and got confused when I see Emilio's face ghost-white.

"What's wrong?" I asked as I wiped my mouth.

"Put your fucking clothes on. Now."

What the hell? Emilio was looking behind me, and when I looked over my shoulder, I saw Aria standing outside his office, holding her shoes.

"Shit," I let out the curse in panic.

"Don't worry about it," Emilio replied as he put his dick back into his pants and adjusted himself.

Quickly grabbing my shirt and bra, I flew out of his office and ran into mine. As I put my clothes on, I was shaking. Will Aria say something? I might as well pack up and leave Chicago before Luca catches wind of this. I was sweating and freaking out. I waited in my office, and eventually, Emilio walked in.

"What did she say?" I impatiently asked.

"Nothing. She didn't care about what she saw; she had other intentions."

"So she's not going to tell Luca?"

"As long as I pull through on a favor, Luca shouldn't find out."

Emilio seemed certain but still looked nervous. I walk up to him and place my hands on his chest, but he removes them.

"You're upset."

"Of course I am, Bethany. Aria will hold this over my head for as long as possible."

"She doesn't come off as the type to do that."

"You don't know that," he said. He took a deep breath. "We need to stop."

"Are you being serious? You were begging for my mouth around your cock." I shake my head and grab my purse.

"If Aria tells Luca, I'm done for.," Emilio replied.

"Luca always gets the upper hand," I roll my eyes in frustration.

"Stop being a child, Bethany."

The fact he called me a child enraged me. "Fine. If you don't want this anymore, then stay the hell away from me."

I've never left the office so fast before. As I drove home, my phone rang. It was Luca. The sight of his name on my phone made me shiver. Trying to send his call to voicemail while driving, I accidentally hit the answer button.

"Where are you?" Luca asked, sounding annoyed.

"Heading home. What's up?"

I held my breath, hoping Aria didn't tell him anything.

"I can't get a hold of Emilio. Was he still in the office?"

"I think so."

There was a pause, "He's on the other line calling me back. Keep your day open tomorrow."

"Why?"

"I want Aria to have a relaxing day. Her brother's hearing will get pushed up. I'm sure it won't sit well with her. I need you to take her out. Distract her somehow and get her mind off it."

I breathed a sigh of relief. "Sure."

"Good, come to the house in the morning."

Getting off the phone with Luca, I felt like I just got away with murder. Now I understood why Emilio was on edge about Aria holding this over his head. We would be on eggshells for as long as Aria was around to tell Luca about what she saw.

I wasn't sure how to look at her after what she saw. But I knew I needed to play extra nice with her.

Chapter 35

That morning, I acted like yesterday didn't happen, and Aria did the same. Not once did she mention what she saw. Hopefully, this was a good sign. We went shopping and spent time bonding, just as my brother requested. Luca even paid for everything. I thought I was a heavy spender, but Aria was on another level.

"Any good spas around here?" Aria asked.

"De Kuyper is really good," I shout over the curtain from the dressing room.

"A massage would be the perfect way to end the day."

"Call them and ask for Pete. That man is a god with his hands."

Aria called to make an appointment.

"They are booked," she said. "But this spa seems nice. It's a new place, and there are two slots open."

"I've never been there."

"Scared?" she asked.

"I'm going to be honest with you, so don't judge."

She laughs, "Try me."

"I've never gone to a place my brother hasn't approved."

Aria laughs again. "Controlling much?"

It made me feel like I grew up in a bubble. Didn't she grow up in the lifestyle too? Why does this sound bizarre to her?

"More like a safety thing, or so he claims," I reply.

"How about I call Emilio to let him know."

"Emilio wouldn't approve that." I poke my head out.

"I think I can get him to," she winked at me.

"Okay," I agreed, knowing what her tactic would be. The more I thought about it, the more I felt obligated to do whatever Aria wanted. If I wasn't in this bind, there was no way we would be going to a spa that wasn't under my brother's control.

Within minutes, Aria got off the phone. "We got the okay!"

I lay face down, mostly naked, under the thin white sheet, waiting for the masseuse to come in. The sound of the door opening and shutting with a woman's voice asking whether I wanted lavender, eucalyptus, or jasmine oil.

"Eucalyptus," I reply. "Can you mix that with mint?"

Even though I was upset with Emilio, I felt this odd need to be around him, and the closest thing was to pick a scent that reminded me of him.

"Sure. I seem to be out of mint. Let me go drop another bottle," the woman said before leaving the room.

Getting impatient waiting, when the door opens, I hold my tongue to avoid commenting. A chill ran through me when a hand ran up my leg, and the sheet was removed from my body.

"What the hell?!" I shouted as I scrambled to look over my shoulder. Managing to turn onto my back, I held the sheet at my chest. Only wearing panties, I felt my nipple harden against the sheet as the scent of eucalyptus and mint invaded my nose.

"You haven't returned my call." Emilio slowly walks toward the table by my feet, dragging his finger up my leg. Even with the sheet as a barrier, my skin was on fire, and my body reacted against my will.

"Oh, now you want to fuck?" I spat out. "Rachel, get boring for you? Is Grace not in town?"

"You're going to tell me you don't want me?"

"I don't," I lied through my teeth.

"Liar."

"I'm not lying. Fucking other women to my face isn't the kind of foreplay I enjoy."

"Just me is enough, isn't it?" that look was in his eyes, making him look like a predator hunting their prey. His hand was gliding up my leg.

"Don't think so highly of yourself." Shifting my leg so that I couldn't feel his touch.

It was tortuous being attracted to such an emotionless man.

Emilio smirked, "The moment my hand made contact with you, you were turned on."

"Not at all," I wasn't lying. I was turned on the moment I laid eyes on him.

Ripping the sheet off of me, he calmly said, "I bet you're wet right now. Am I right?'

"Dry as a bone."

"Should I check if you're lying?"

My gig was up when he placed his hand on my thigh and glided it over my thin lace underwear to my core. Even I could feel the moisture spill through the fabric as he placed pressure against it. He propped his other hand onto the table, leaning close to my face.

Remaining still with my hands on the table supporting my upper body as I slightly leaned back, I was getting lightheaded. Pushing aside my panty line with one finger, he inserts a finger inside of me. Widening my legs, giving him more access, he slides in another. I bite my lower lip to hold back, making any kind of pleasurable noise as though that would give me away. Not that it made any difference. By this point, I was soaking, and the sound of his fingers entering inside and out of me against the wetness filled the room. The bed under me was wet. We were both watching each other as I tried my best not to make a sound while he remained at a steady tempo, fingering me.

"Another one?" he whispered.

I nod my head eagerly, and in goes another finger. This caused me to lift my pelvis for him to go deeper. Emilio wraps his free hand around my hair and grabs the top of my ponytail, pulling it back and causing me to tilt my head back. Examining my face, he leaned in so close that our noses touched. Lightly, he brushed his nose against mine as the fingers inside me curved as they glided in and out. The simple act had me panting. He edged closer, and our lips were about to touch. My breath picked up as my heartbeat was thumping out of my chest. Was he going to kiss me? The thought alone was causing me to orgasm, and my lips quivered as I let out a soft moan.

His tongue traced my lip, and there was a look in his eyes that I'd never seen before, a look of calmness. As he was going to place his lips onto mine, there was a disruptive outburst outside the room. Quickly, Emilio stood up straight, and the sound of someone screaming to call 911 quickly had him remove his fingers from inside me and let my ponytail go free from his grip.

"Get dressed," he demanded as he grabbed his gun. "Wait in here."

I watch him storm out, shutting the door behind him. What was going on? I quickly threw on my clothes and waited for someone to get me, but the sound of a gun outside the room had me in a panic. Quickly scanning the room, I hide in one of the towel closets, squeezing myself into the tiny space. Just as I was able to close most of the closet door, the door to the room swung open, and in walked a man. He was dressed in black pants, shoes, and a button-down. I was able to see through the cracks. He quickly undressed and threw on my spa robe as though pretending to be a guest. Before fully putting it on, I get a glimpse of his back and see a familiar birthmark on his left shoulder. It's the same birthmark from the man at the sex club I was eagerly trying to run into months ago.

A man walks in looking like someone who works here. "Boss, the car is ready out back. We need to leave now."

He nodded his head, "As long as no one will suspect anything."

"We are all cleared."

They both leave wearing attire that would blend them into the crowd around here. A chill ran down my spine. Once they left, I busted out of the closet and headed for the door, but it opened it again. This time it was Emilio.

"What's going on?" I ask in a panic.

"Aria is passed out in the other room with burn marks."

"What?! How?"

"I'm going to look into it. Right now I need you to stay with her in the other room. The spa called an ambulance, so you need to go to the hospital with her. I'll meet you there with your brother."

"He's not going to be happy about this."

"We need to get our story straight," Emilio fixed his suit jacket. "I'm supposed to be across town right now. So wait 15 minutes before you call him. I'll text him now that I'm heading back into the area."

"Why am I calling Luca?" I could feel the sweat form on my body.

"Because I'm off the radar. So if you called me first, I wouldn't have answered. But his call I would."

I nod my head in understanding. "Is she going to be okay?"

"She'll be fine. The burns weren't too deep."

"Good, I'll see you in the hospital then."

Emilio opened his mouth to say something, but nothing came out. He had turned around for a second but then turned back and pulled me into him. It took me by surprise, but what shocked me more was when he kissed me. It wasn't a peck or just a lips-to-lips kind of kiss. The back of his hand was on my head, pressing it further into his as our tongues danced with one another. I was on cloud 9. When he pulled away, I was breathless.

And in a blink of an eye, he was gone.

Chapter 36

I had to stay in the waiting room until my brother showed up. It was written all over his face that he was livid. Emilio followed closely behind him, scanning the area as they stormed through the hospital, clearing anyone who would question their presence as they disobeyed the protocols put in place.

I got to my feet as he got closer. "The doctor said– "

Before I could get the rest out of my mouth, Luca grabbed my arm and dragged me with him. Slamming me into the wall, he got in my face.

"How did this happen?"

I've seen Luca angry before, but he never took it out on me and was never this aggressive with me.

"She wanted to go to a spa."

His hand slammed the wall beside my head. It made me cringe, but he didn't seem to care. "Then take her to one that I clear. Do you understand the shit I now need to deal with?"

"I–"

"You what?" Luca spat out, cutting me off. Nothing I could say would help the situation. "You fucked up. Big. All I asked was to distract her for the day. You can't even manage that."

My face was getting wet as tears streamed down it. Unable to speak, Luca opened his mouth again, but Emilio approached us, breaking the tension.

"Lorenzo should be here soon."

Luca huffed. "Get the fuck out of my face and go home," he said, dismissing me.

Shaken by my brother's reaction, I run off. Where to, I didn't know. My car wasn't here, and this hospital is huge. Making it out the front, I opened the door to inhale fresh air, but Chicago's hot, humid summers mixed with anxiety made breathing difficult. I stood in the middle of the street, looking like a lost child.

"Bethany."

I turn to find Emilio behind me, "Just leave me alone." I turn back to him, embarrassed that he witnessed what just happened.

He walks to stand beside me, looking forward, "I don't need to explain the situation in detail to you and why your brother is stressed about this."

"It wasn't even my fault," I sniffled.

"I know. It was my fault for allowing it."

"Did she hold what she said against you?"

"No," Emilio replied. "I was being selfish. I wanted to see you and going to that spa was the perfect spot without anyone seeing or reporting back to Luca."

Blushing at his confession, "Do you regret that choice?"

He paused, "I regret not having self-control."

Unsure if that was a backhand compliment, I proceeded to tell him about the man who came into my room. "I saw a man. Not sure if he was involved, but he came into my room, took off his clothes, and put on a robe then walked out."

"Did you get a good look at him?"

I nod my head. "Dark hair, brown eyes. Defined jawline. A birthmark on his left shoulder."

"That's helpful. Now I need to figure out how to bring that up to Luca."

"What's Luca so concerned about anyway? Around Aria, it's like he forgets he's a DeCarlo. We hold the power."

Emilio was silent for a moment. "I think he has genuine feelings for her."

Taken back, I couldn't believe what I was hearing. "Luca catch feelings? Does he even know what feelings are?"

"He is human, Bethany. Cut the man some slack."

"You always take his side." I begin to walk away.

"B, where are you going?"

Talking over my shoulder, "What's it matter to you?"

He caught up to me and grabbed my elbow gently. "Hey. Look at me."

I stop and turn to face him. "It's not fair."

"Life's not fair. You just need to roll with the punches."

"You think he has feelings for Aria?"

Emilio nodded, "It's not an ideal situation."

"Do you think Aria has feelings for him? Genuine feelings?"

Again, nodding his head, "She fights it, but they are there."

"And if they choose to accept those feelings…, would they choose each other?"

"Time will tell. At some point, it will all come crashing down."

Although the conversation was geared toward Aria and Luca, I was referring to us and Emilio was doing the same.

"If they could make it work…" I paused to see Emilio's reaction.

"Don't."

"Why not?"

"It's different. You and I," Emilio shook his head, "it's not the same."

"It's not. It's better."

"Better?" Emilio questioned, but he seemed upset. "Nothing about you and I would make our situation better."

I sighed, "What are you saying, Emilio?"

"You know what I'm saying."

"You're the closest person to my brother. What better person for me to be with?"

"That's the point, Bethany. Each time I think of you, I betray him. Each time I touch you, I betray him."

"It doesn't stop you, though," I reminded him.

"And it eats me up inside. The fact we got caught by someone enrages me. I don't like when people have something to hold over my head."

A ball of emotion was stuck in my throat. Deep down, I knew what it would be like if he had to choose between being with me or my brother's Consigliere.

"So then why keep doing it?" I challenge.

"I don't know."

I spat out regretfully. "Let's just end it now. For good. Pretend it never happened."

Stupidly, a part of me thought he would fight back, but that was a ridiculous belief. With one last blow to the heart, his response sent me into a state of numbness.

"I agree."

Chapter 37

Standing in the shower as the hot water stung my skin, turning it red, it took everything within me to stop sobbing. I have been feeling numb since leaving the hospital yesterday; nothing seemed to matter anymore. How am I able to cry without emotion? My heart was ripped out, and I just didn't understand why I was always the one put on the sidelines. Eventually, I leave the burning water and throw on some clothes. My phone had ten missed calls from Alfie and counting. No matter who they were, I was in no mood to talk to anyone.

I was ready to be my own person, but to do that, I needed to leave Chicago. How would I be able to look at Emilio without breaking down? Something needs to change—I need to change. So, I began plotting where I'd go, when, and how I would survive. With a degree in business management, I could find something. Maybe I'd go to a small town and make some friends that would turn into family. Isn't that what Aria did? Ugh. The thought of her was upsetting me. I envied her in more ways than one. She was smart—the kind of smart that can keep up with Luca's kind—she was bold, unafraid to stand up for herself, and how she chose a life she wanted for herself were all things I didn't have in me.

To no surprise, there was a knock at the door. Someone was here to check up on me, but I wasn't interested in playing along anymore. I don't know if I ever would if I didn't step up now. Lounging on the sofa, I was on my laptop, looking up homes in small cities. The knocking on the door became louder, and I continued to ignore it. My phone starts to ring. It was Luca. His behavior was so belligerent yesterday I didn't want to see him. If that's the kind of behavior that Aria, a Cassariano, sparked within him to speak to his own flesh and blood, then why have any respect for him in return?

The call drops, and then he calls again. He calls three more times before sending a text message.

> **Luca D.**
>
> Please answer the door. I need to speak with you.
>
> Why? So you can degrade me again?
>
> B, I'm sorry. I was wrong for lashing out at you like that.

I had to read that over again a few times. Was Luca apologizing? Am I hallucinating? Getting off the sofa, I go to let him in. When I opened the door, the sight of him got me worried. Never in my life have I ever seen my brother look unsettled.

"Are you okay?" I asked as I let him in.

Luca was silent and just walked in. Unlike the usual attire of a three-piece, he wore a regular suit with the top two buttons undone. Walking into my kitchen, he pulls out a bottle of liquor from my cabinet. He's a scotch drinker, but I'm not. The strongest thing I got was Dulce Vida Blanco tequila. Watching him pour himself a shot and down it like water made me question what could have my brother this rattled.

"This is fucking garbage," he said before taking another shot.

"You should slow down; that's 50% proof." I walked over and took the bottle away after he poured a third shot. "Okay, you're freaking me out now. What's up with you?"

Luca just stared at the shot while he leaned on the countertop with his two hands for support. "I needed to speak to someone who wouldn't be judgmental."

My heart tightened. His words made me miss the bond Luca and I used to have before power consumed him. I don't remember when it happened, but it was like a switch. One day, we were as close as possible, telling each other everything about our personal lives to suddenly every little thing he said and did affected every part of his life, which only made him grow cold toward me.

"I'm all ears," I replied.

"Aria is pregnant." Luca never took his eyes off the shot in front of him. "And it might not be mine."

Jesus, minutes ago, I envied her, and now I wasn't sure what to think.

"It might not be yours?" I questioned.

Luca grabbed the shot in front of him and downed it. "She's been sleeping with her business partner."

"Wow," I blurted out unintentionally.

Luca gave me a look, "What happened to no judgment?"

I took a deep breath, "Sorry. She just seems to have it all together. Seems like a silly slip-up. When did she tell you?"

"She didn't," he motioned for me to hand him the bottle, "Emilio knows the nurse from the hospital. That's how we found out."

I placed the bottle far from Luca's reach. "So now what? You're going to pretend you don't know?"

"I'm going to force it out of her."

"How do you plan to do that?"

"If I put us all in the same room, I can get her to crack."

"Okay. What makes you think she would have her business partner come to Chicago?"

"He arrived last night."

My eyes widened, "She has no shame." When he shot me another look, I held my hand up in surrender, "Sorry. This is a lot. Do you want it to be yours?"

Luca didn't reply; he just walked over to the bottle and took a swing.

He nods his head as though that was an acceptable answer. He was torn, but it wasn't because he was unsure. Luca wanted the baby to be his, and if it wasn't, that meant he couldn't have Aria.

"Luca, do you have feelings for her?"

He was going to take another gulp from the bottle but then realized the alcohol was getting to him, so he placed it back onto the countertop.

"I don't want to," he replied.

"But you do."

"She changed everything, B." The look in his eyes told me it was the truth. "I thought after Sandra, I'd never feel love for another woman the way I loved her. Then, after the first time seeing Aria, without even speaking to her, I sold off the vineyard just to get her in front of me."

It hurt me to see him talking about his first love. Sandra was the kindest person I had ever encountered and was taken from him. He named a vineyard after her and would say he would only sell it when he moved on.

"If you are the father," I questioned, "Then what? She is still a Cassariano."

"I'd marry her."

Luca was a widow. His wife Claire was an arranged marriage. When she passed away, he swore never to marry again. So, for him to marry Aria without hesitation spoke volumes.

"A Cassariano? What happened to not crossing boundaries? Her family killed our brother. No one will look past it."

"It's complicated."

"Of course, it is," I huffed.

No matter how irritating it was to hear it, I knew everything little thing was complicated. Luca's every move needed to be calculated to avoid costing him something or someone. I let out a deep breath. Walking over to him, I give him a huge hug.

Returning the hug, Luca said, "You know I love you, right? I lost my temper and was harsh on you."

"Glad you can admit to that." Pulling out of the hug, I take the bottle and place it back into the cabinet so he won't have anymore. "Can you admit to something else?" I questioned.

"Depends."

"Would you ever approve of me being with someone in your inner circle?"

Luca was taken aback, "Like who?"

I shrug, "Anyone."

Luca gave me a look. "I'd need to know who before I could answer that. Why are you asking?"

I had to think of an excuse. "Just curious."

"I don't like the idea of it. Gives everyone else a sense of favoritism. That never goes over well."

"What if I told you I want to leave Chicago?"

"And go where?"

"Anywhere."

Luca laughed, "No. You're safest in Chicago."

I've been told I needed to stay in the city because my family would never have to worry about my safety the way they would if I left Chicago.

"So I can't just live my life how I want?"

Luca started holding onto the counter as though he would fall. Pulling his phone out, he makes a call.

"Pick me up. I'm at Bethany's." He hangs up and begins walking toward the living room.

"Who did you call?"

"Emilio. He will be here soon." As he continued to walk away, he shouted over his shoulder, "Oh, and the answer to your question. It's a no."

When there was a knock at the door, my nerves spiked up. I knew if I looked through the peephole and saw Emilio, I wouldn't be able to open the door. So I held my breath and swung the door open, only to find someone else standing there.

"Alfie?"

"Hey, B." He walks in. "Emilio said your brother is here and needs a ride."

"Aren't you supposed to be flying back to California?"

"Last minute change of plans."

Although Luca wasn't able to drive, he was able to walk just fine. I watched them walk out and shut the door behind them. My brother told me I was stuck here forever. Which means I'm stuck at his beck and call. It made me sick to my stomach.

If I wanted to break free, I'd have to do this on my own. That meant cutting all ties with my name. Spending the day planning out my new life, my stomach started to growl. I order dinner and pop a bottle of wine while I wait for my food. A long time ago, Luca had separate identities created for each of us in case we needed to go on the run.

Pulling it out from my safe, I look at the social security card, a passport, a birth certificate, and an entire new life planned out in a folder. It was now or never.

Chapter 38

I spent a week pretending everything was fine. I wasn't upset; I made it a point to spend time with my mother and sisters out of guilt that I wouldn't tell them goodbye. My brother and Emilio were heading to New York on the spur of the moment. This was my shot. The first thing I did was empty my bank account and do some wire transfers so I had the funds to survive until I got my new life on track. The next thing I did was go to Luca's house.

"Hey Albert," I said, "Give this to Luca when he returns."

He nodded and took the envelope from me. Inside the envelope was a letter I wrote explaining how I was okay and not to find me. My last call was to deactivate my phone. Taking a deep breath, I drive off, heading toward Arizona. Waiting for me, there was a home I purchased within a newly built community in a small town. 26 hours later, I was driving up to my new place to start a new life. My mother must be worried sick. My sisters are probably nagging Luca to find me. And Luca himself, I'm sure he is livid.

The air here was different and something I had to get used to. I spent two weeks adjusting before I started getting homesick. I started job searching and got an interview scheduled for this little business. It went well, and I was proud of getting something without using the name DeCarlo.

Walking into a coffee shop, I wait in line to order my drink.

"Bethany?" a man's voice said.

The sound of my name stunned me. I was semi-adjusting to people calling me by my new name, but to hear my real name called was a mind twist. Choosing to ignore it, I didn't move.

"Bethany, is that you?"

I could see from the corner of my eye that the person was approaching me. Sweat started forming on my forehead, and I was ready to run out of there.

"It's me, Nate Reilly."

I wasn't sure if that was a good thing or not. Without having much of a choice, I turn to face him.

"Hey! Nate, what are you doing here?"

"Business trip," he smiled. "What are you doing here?"

"Vacation," I lied.

"Nate," a woman came over and placed her arm around his.

It was Veronica Merrill. By the look of them, it seemed like they were together. Was Aria aware of this or do people from California just enjoy sleeping with multiple people openly?

"Veronica, this is Bethany DeCarlo. Bethany, this is my colleague, Veronica Merrill."

"Yes, I know Bethany," Veronica smiled. "I've done work for Luca De-Carlo. That is her brother."

Nate looked uncomfortable.

"Look, I need to run. Hope you enjoyed your coffee!" I sprinted out of there, and my heart raced as I headed home.

My cover was blown. I knew it'd be a matter of time before my brother sent someone to get me, so I knew I needed to get out of there fast. It was disappointing that I barely got to live here, and now I needed to think of somewhere else. Walking into my house, I throw my keys down and reach for my laptop.

"Why Arizona?" Emilio's voice behind me made me scream in fear.

"Why not?" I shot back as I turned to face him, breathing heavily from the shock.

As soon as I saw his face, my heart felt like it was being ripped apart again. He looked upset as he stood there looking at me. I wouldn't ask how he found me before Veronica could mention anything. I'm sure I did something to flag them where I was.

"Do you know how I needed to talk your brother off the ledge from him coming here himself to drag you back home? He let this carry out longer than he wanted, thinking you'd come to your senses and return."

I gulp, "I don't want to go home."

"You don't have much of a choice."

Tears built up in my eyes and started streaming down my face. At this point, what did I have to lose? I pour my heart out at one final attempt to win him over. "If I can't be with you, then I can't be around you."

"I'm not the kind of person you want to be with. There's someone out there better. Made just for you."

"It's always, 'You'll find someone better.' That there's this 'so good the rest don't matter' type of love."

Emilio furrowed his brows, "You deserve a real love, Bethany."

"Why can't it be from you?"

"That's just not me."

"You rather lose me?"

"Bethany, I'm not losing you. I'm letting you get away."

"And you're willing to live with that?"

"I've lived with worse. I mourned the death of the man I was before taking this title. Any hope for saving my soul was lost. But in becoming the man I am now, some losses were worth the grief. Maybe you'll learn that lesson one day. We both know this isn't going to work."

"But what if it does? It is not worth finding out?" I plead. "Am I not worth it?"

Letting out a deep breath, "I never said that."

"Then what are you saying?" When he wouldn't answer, I kept pushing. "Well. Am I nothing to you?"

"I'll wait in the car for you," he replied, walking out.

I am stomping behind him. "Answer me. Emilio!"

"WHAT!?" He angrily turned around and shouted. I've never seen him lose his cool before. "What do you want from me? You knew from the start what this would be... what this could only be."

"I love you," I said aloud, thinking I'd regret it, but I didn't.

He didn't want to hear it, but I had to put it out there. He had to know. Part of me hoped it was enough for him to change his mind.

"No, you don't."

"Yes, I do."

"You don't know me, Bethany."

"How can you say that?"

"You know one version of me. One."

I place my hands on my hip. "You're being ridiculous. Just making things up to change my mind, but you can't."

"I'm not trying to change your mind. You know one side of me."

"And it's the most personal side of you. That has to mean something."

Emilio shook his head. "You would hate the other side of me, Bethany. The side of me that keeps the DeCarlo Family going. The side of me that resents my past. The side of me that would do anything to protect you."

"I would love every version of you." A teardrop fell down my face.

"Every version of me doesn't even love me. I can deal with that. But you," he shook his head, "I couldn't. You can't truly have me without the madness that makes me. And trust me, Bethany, it's not worth risking everything for."

I drop my arms to my side in defeat. "So that's it?"

"This is it, Bethany," he replied without any emotion.

Before Emilio could turn away, I blurt out, "Just one more time."

"One more time what?"

"Own me. Just one last time."

Chapter 39

"Own me. Just one last time."

The words came out of my mouth with such eagerness. Emilio stood there unsure at first but then began removing his jacket and tie. I follow his lead, quickly undressing myself. No matter how fast we moved, it didn't seem fast enough. Our naked bodies collided; Emilio grabbed my jaw and pulled my mouth onto his. Our mouths crashed together, and our souls felt connected as we gave into one another for the last time. If time could standstill to make this moment last longer, it still wouldn't be enough. Without breaking away, our mouths devoured one another, and as each moment was savored, I couldn't help the ball of emotion within me. Emilio slaps his hands on my bare ass, lifting me so that I could wrap my legs around him. I lock my ankles as he slams my back against the wall. His hands pin my wrists beside my head as his body presses against mine.

Emilio begins trailing kisses along my jawline toward my ear and down to my mid-neck, where he concentrates on nibbling. My hand on the opposite side finds its way to my breast, grabbing and twisting my nipple. Taking my free hand to place on his chest, I could feel his heart beating hard. Sliding my hand further down, I reach for his cock. In rhythm, I stroke his hardening shaft as he twists my nipple. The warmth of Emilio's breath, as he continued to suck, lick, and nibble on my neck, was making me breathe heavier. Letting go of my other hand, I wrap my arm around his neck for support while his hand makes its way to my core, sliding two fingers inside. Everything was in sync, and I was on cloud 9. Tilting my head back, I began breathing heavier. Removing his mouth from my neck, he moved on to my other breast. I felt like I was on edge, but I knew I needed to hold out and wait for Emilio's command.

The pre cum from the head of his penis spilled onto my hand and served as a lube as I continued to stroke his shaft up and down. I could feel my own wetness coming out of me. Letting out a cry of pleasure from the burn of his bite on my nipple made me grip his erection harder. Lifting his head, our mouths collided once again, and both his hands grabbed my thighs. My free arm wraps around his neck, locking hands with the one already there as Emilio places me on the floor.

The cold wood against my skin made me arc my back, throwing my breasts up into his face. Rather than ravish them, he takes it all in as though trying to engrave the sight into his memory. He hovered over me while balancing himself on his forearms. Our eyes met, and the usual hunger there was replaced by a look of softness that I'd never thought I'd see. Before it could choke me up, I felt him enter inside of me. Usually, Emilio pushes himself fully inside of me all at once without being gentle. This was a different experience as I felt every inch of him filling up my inside slowly. I thought I was about to cum right there, but I knew better.

"Bethany," Emilio breathed as he slowly pumped in and out of me.

"I know," I reply, exhaling.

A smirk crossed his face. I knew how he liked it. The need for us to finish simultaneously felt crucial, like it was the proper ending to our chapter. Keeping a steady pace going in and out, he went deeper each time, causing an orgasm to begin bubbling within me. The intoxicating pleasure felt like my body was breaking into a million pieces. Emilio began moving his hip forward quicker, and the steady pace was now turning into forceful strikes, his momentum unwavering. I loved every hit. I was panting as I tightened my legs around him to the point of pain and dug my nails into his back as though holding on for my dear life. Every back muscle clenched as he let out a growl. Heaving and sweating, he shifts his hands to grab under my thighs and lifts them so that his cock hits a different angle inside of me. Emilio is unforgiving as he repeatedly drives into me, losing all control of himself as his body collapses onto mine. My mind is spiraling from the tension building. His fingers flex on my thighs, gripping them as though he was holding on to ensure I wouldn't just disappear.

The sound of our bodies colliding echoed in the room. The inside of my core starts to tighten, and I give Emilio a look. There is no way I would be able to hold back anymore. His breathing is harsh in my ear, and our sweat-ridden bodies are flush and heaving severely. He groans as he circles his hips as he remains deep inside of me.

"Are you ready for me, sweetheart?" his husky voice in my ear made me dig my nails further into his back.

I nod in desperation. Emilio lifts his body and stands on his knees in front of me—my legs still wrapped around him. Pulling his erection out and then slamming it back in made me dizzy. Aggressively pounding into me, I close my eyes, throwing my back in a desperate scream.

"Look at me," he demanded.

Forcing my eyes open, we looked at one another, and when Emilio nodded, I let the explosion rupture through me. I'm knocked out by a climax that rushes forward so fast I thought my soul left my body. Emilio lets out a groan and falls forward back onto me. We both were breathless as we lay there sweaty, slowly coming off that high. Lifting his head, he looked into my eyes as though he wanted to say something. When no words left his mouth, I opened mine.

"I love you," I say with confidence.

"Bethany–" he whispered.

"You don't have to love me back. I just need you to know how I feel."

Placing a kiss on my forehead, Emilio then gets up to get dressed. Pure silence. It hurt more than I thought it would, but I did this to myself. To expect a different outcome wouldn't just be childish but selfish of me. This wasn't what he wanted—I wasn't what he wanted.

It was time to accept that.

Chapter 40

The plane ride from Arizona to Illinois was quiet. Using my brother's jet plane, Emilio and I sat across from one another in a dead eye lock as the plane made its way down the lane and into the sky. The silence felt deadly, and I turned my focus to look outside the window hoping it would clear my mind. Never in all my time have I ever wanted something so badly and couldn't have it at the same time. I thought it was one of those 'you want what you can't have phases,' but that was far from it. Somehow, I managed to catch feelings for a man who not only I can't have but also doesn't want me in return.

My mouth was still red from the intense mouth-to-mouth back in the house, and I felt noticeably disheveled while Emilio appeared calm and collected. Not a piece of clothing out of place. With his elbow propped onto the armrest, he held his jaw with his thumb and pointer, appearing to be in deep thought; his knee brushed against mine, grabbing my attention.

When our eyes met, a lump in my throat formed. How was I ever going to be able to look at Emilio with a normal face? The tears bunched in my eyes, causing me to look away again.

"A pretty lady like you shouldn't be crying."

I felt something placed in my hands that I had held together on my lap. Looking down, I was a handkerchief, which only made this sting more.

"How are you still carrying these?"

"I'm old, remember?" he smiled.

Taking it from him, Emilio brushed his finger against my skin.

"You're going to taunt me forever?"

"That's not what I'm trying to do," Emilio replied.

I looked at him as he leaned forward with each elbow on his knees.

"Then stop being nice," I said.

"I've always been kind to you. That doesn't need to change."

"I can't just go back to how things were with you. How do you expect me just to forget the nights we spent together and pretend they never existed? To erase all of it from my memory? How?"

"You just do." Emilio exhaled a deep breath as he sat up straight.

"My brother is holding you back."

"He should be holding you back as well."

"That's how you're going to live your life?"

"There are limits, Bethany. No one gets everything without facing the consequences."

"At least I had the courage to lose myself in something I wanted."

I got to my feet and sat in another seat so that he was out of sight for the remainder of the flight.

———

Waking up to the plane landing, Emilio was already on the phone before the plane door opened. When he got off, he looked at me with a grave face.

"Your brother wants me to take you to him."

There was a knot in my stomach. The entire flight, I could only focus on my anger with Emilio for not choosing me. I didn't even think about the wrath that Luca would bestow on me. Remaining silent, we both sat in the back of the Escalade. Looking out the window, it seemed we were headed away from the city.

"Where are you taking us?" Emilio asked.

The driver looked at him through the rearview mirror, "Mr. DeCarlo wants me to take you both to the spot."

I didn't have any clue as to where this spot was, but Emilio seemed annoyed. Everything was fine until there was no road, and the car was driving onto a dirt pathway. We arrive in the middle of who knows where and find my brother with Alfie and another man.

"What the fuck is going on?" Emilio asked out loud to himself as he exited the car.

Slowly, I get out and walk up to them, confused. Luca looked livid, as expected. Alfie looked concerned. The man beside them seemed amused. It was humid out, my clothes sticking to my body. How they were able to wear suits in this weather was insane. Behind them was an old 1970 Chevelle SS that had dirt and dust all over it.

"Cahill," Emilio shakes the man's hand.

"Emilio," he smiles, "Good to see you." He had a thick Irish accent.

"What brings you to Chicago?" Emilio glances at Luca.

My brother clears his throat, "You know Riley likes to make surprise visits." Luca makes eye contact with me. "Bethany. Glad you're back. Are you done with your little stunt?"

I could feel this strange tension, and the attention on me made me nervous. "I'm done."

The focus then went to Emilio. "Emilio, you've been slipping up on me," Luca told him.

Hiding any kind of panic that I could imagine he was feeling, Emilio replied, "How so?"

"I've asked you to keep closer tabs on Bethany lately."

It felt like the air escaped my lungs; in its place was the humidity, making me lightheaded.

"Which I have been," Emilio confessed.

"Bethany," Luca said. "Where have you been spending your free time?"

His question almost had me faint. The beads of sweat formed on my forehead as I struggled to find something to say.

"Home mostly," I answer.

"That's not what I heard."

In full panic mode, I remained silent, unsure how to respond. Luca snapped his finger, which made Alfie pop open the trunk and pull out a man tied up, letting him fall to the ground.

The man's face was bloody, so I couldn't make out who it was, but he was begging for help through the cloth shoved into his mouth. Alfie kicks him in the which causes him to wince in pain.

"Bethany," Luca said, "Do you remember his man?"

"No," I was nervous.

"I thought you'd have more class than this," Luca spat out. "Alfie's friend Mark works at the mayor's office. This prick was bragging about landing some hot blonde at a sex party. If it weren't for Alfie's birthday picture on his desk, it wouldn't have gotten out that he was referring to you."

It felt as though I was burning at the stake. The man on the floor was Dillan from the sex party, but I didn't go home with him or do anything sexual. It was the night Emilio dragged me out.

Luca said, "Emilio have you heard of those sex parties?"

"I have," again he confessed.

"Have you gone to any?"

"Once or twice."

"Have you ever seen Bethany at any of them?"

Emilio paused before answering, "I have."

There was no way Emilio would lie to my brother. That's the number one rule to being a Consigliere. Luca looked ready to rip his head off. Countless times, Emilio has saved my ass without expecting anything in return. This was my turn. So, I had to cut in.

"I didn't fuck the guy if that's what you're getting at." I held my breath, hoping to distract my brother from focusing on Emilio.

"That's supposed to make me feel better?" Luca replied to me, then turned his focus back to Emilio. "Why wouldn't you tell me something like that, Emilio?"

"You had a lot on your plate. Hosting a Cassariano, dealing with the Appollo brothers—the last thing you needed to worry about was Bethany at a party she didn't belong. Like all the other things, I handled it without further problems."

Luca stepped closer to him, "You should have said something at some point."

I cut in to take away the tension from Emilio, "I begged him not to. I was embarrassed, and I promised not to do it again."

"I'm supposed to believe it didn't happen again?" Luca wasn't convinced.

"I learned my lesson," I plead. "After he spiked my drink, I– "

"Spiked your drink?" Luca repeated.

I gulp, "Yes. Emilio saw me just in time."

Luca looked to Emilio, who nodded in agreement.

"It wasn't worth the stress," Emilio added, "But it won't happen again. You have my word—regardless of what it is, I'll inform you immediately."

Luca took a deep breath. "You made a judgment call. I respect that. But don't let something like that slip again." He turned to Dillon, who was on the floor. "The prick drugged her; what do you think we should do?"

"We should teach him a lesson," Emilio encouraged.

Luca smiled, "That we should."

Riley Cahill had a smirk on his face, "Ah, you Chicago fellas know how to make me smile."

"Tie him up, Alfie," Luca commanded.

We watch as Dillon gets tied up to the back bumper of the car. Alfie then gets into the vehicle and drives off, dragging the man behind him. His screams gave me goosebumps. The look of horror was all over my face. I tense as Luca walks toward me.

He whispers, "Just know you're responsible for that. Your reckless behavior put that person in this position. He's lucky Emilio came in before something worse happened."

"I'm sorry," I whisper back.

"Your sorries become less meaningful each time you need to say them. And if you ever think of running away again, I'll put you in the damn box and lock you in there for just as long as you've been away for."

Chapter 41

My brother sat there puffing on his cigar as a handful of men seated with him at the table playing poker. Emilio was standing off to the side, just watching. I've been on house arrest for over a week, and I was starting to get cabin fever. This was the first time I saw Emilio since he dragged me back to Chicago. He had distanced himself so far from me that I barely got a hello. There was no official goodbye parting, just an absence. A sudden abrupt absence louder than any voice could be.

The room was full of cigar smoke and the smell of bourbon. Standing at the table, I clear my throat.

"Luca."

My brother glances up at me as I stand opposite the table. "What are you doing here?"

"I have a proposal for you."

This made Emilio walk closer to the table, standing behind Luca. Both of them waited for me to speak.

"What is it?" Luca asked, uninterested.

"Hamilton Branton."

Luca raised his head from his deck of cards and looked at me. "The D.A.'s son. What about him?"

"Arrange a marriage with him."

Shocked, Luca asked, "Why should I do that?"

"He's the D.A.'s son."

Luca looked back down at the deck of cards. "I already have the D.A. in my pocket."

"For now." I stood tall, confident in my words.

He was looking back up to me. "For now?" he repeated, urging me to continue.

"The Branton family are political legacies. There is no doubt that Hamilton will be the successor to his father."

"That's up to the people of Chicago," Luca shot back.

"And we know how the people of Chicago vote," implying the obvious. "So when Hamilton takes his father's place, you'll need him on your side."

"Except arranging this will mean I owe the D.A. and I don't like owing anyone. The point of having someone in your pocket means you have control over them, not the other way around. I don't see this working in my favor."

I look down in defeat. Part of Luca must have felt bad for me. Since Aria found out she was pregnant, she has been in New York figuring things out. They should know who the father is any day now, so Luca has been in a mood. The whole situation had him on his feet, and I was convinced that was why he went easy on me—or maybe my mother and sisters put pressure on him to be kinder to me.

"Then pick someone," I request.

"Pick someone?" Luca was holding back from laughing. "Last time I had arranged something for you, you threatened to kill yourself."

Taking a deep breath and exhaling, I nod my head. "Take it as a plea to get back in your good graces."

Luca observed me and realized I wasn't kidding.

"Everyone, leave," he stated. Everyone but Emilio left the room. "Emilio, remember what we spoke about the other day?"

"I do," he replied.

"Bethany would make a good match."

"It would be more convincing than the match with Gabe."

Luca paused to think, then nodded his head. "How can we convince Gian Morrechi to marry his nephew to Bethany?"

Morrechi was the third most powerful family in the country under us, DeCarlos and the Baricellis. They were based out of Connecticut.

"I have blackmail on the kid," Emilio replied, not looking at me.

Luca glances at Emilio, who has moved into his line of vision. "What kind of blackmail?"

"Something he wouldn't want anyone to know. Or the Morrechi himself, for that matter."

"Like what?"

"The kid is into pegging. Not very good reputation for anyone in this lifestyle."

"What the fuck is pegging?" Luca asked.

Emilio leaned in and whispered into his ear. Seeing my brother's expression, I had to hold back from laughing.

"He's a sick bastard," Luca said in disgust. "You got proof?"

"I do."

"How did you come about this information?"

"I had the blonde get it on film when he came to visit Chicago a short time ago."

The blonde? Who was he referring to?

"She pegged him?"

Emilio laughed, "You want the details?"

"No," Luca replied.

"Grace is good at what she does."

Grace. The blonde. It clicked. She was coming out of Emilio's condo that night. It wasn't him that she was messing with. She was just dropping off the evidence. Emilio was always a step ahead and had something up his sleeve ready to be used to their advantage.

Luca's interest was piqued. "B, are you sure?"

I nod my head. "I'm sure."

It wasn't like me to agree blindly to something like this, but it was better than being stuck in this limbo period with Luca. I was just hoping the guy was half-good-looking, and although his sexual experiences are different from what I prefer, I think I can manage. The pegging would have to be done by someone else, though. That, for me, was crossing the line.

"Set it up," Luca stated to Emilio.

"Consider it done." Emilio got to his feet and left the room without so much as looking at me.

He didn't pay me any attention. I expected him to fight the decision or make another suggestion, but no, he would let this marriage happen. And just like that, I felt my heart break again. Why do my expectations get the best of me?

"I like this change, B. It suits you."

"You mean being heartless."

Luca shook his head, "It's not about being heartless. It's learning how to use your heart less."

"What good will that do me?"

"Gives me peace of mind that you'll be okay."

I roll my eyes, "Why wouldn't I be okay?"

"You never know. I may not be around forever."

Shifting in my seat, "Why are you saying that?"

"It's true. I can be here tomorrow and gone the next."

As if I wasn't emotional enough, his words almost brought me to tears. "You wouldn't let that happen. You have Antonio. Me. The whole family leans on you. You are Luca DeCarlo."

"I'm going to be straight with you, B." Luca looked serious. "Being at the top doesn't always mean things are easier. So, never think that you're safe. Look at what happened to Aria at the spa."

"Was the guy caught?"

"It was more than one person. Emilio told me that you happened to see one of them. Are you sure you know what you saw?"

"I do," I replied. "I'll never forget that birthmark."

Luca looked uneasy. "The description you gave matched a particular person, but it's impossible for it to be that them."

"How come?"

"They're dead."

"Oh," I replied, unsure how to process that.

"But it shouldn't concern you. Someone was after Aria, which means you're still safe."

"But Aria isn't, and if that baby is yours, then neither are they."

I could see the anguish in Luca.

"If that child is mine, I've already failed it. Like Liliana and potentially Antonio."

"Liliana wasn't your fault, Luca. And Antonio is doing so well for himself already."

"It doesn't matter, B. Antonio will always have to look over his shoulder even though I've made it possible for him not to take the same path I have. Until I take my last breath on this earth, my family will always be subjected to the unknown."

"The cycle can't be broken," I conclude.

"Not on our level. It's not about power for me; it's about survival."

Chapter 42

Rehearsal dinner was at the most exclusive restaurant in Chicago. My family looked so proud of this marriage. It was better this way. Pio Morrechi was a good-looking man with a promising future ahead of him. It was an alliance based on my consent. I could still live comfortably while this marriage benefitted my family. Luca was securing a tie to the Morrechi Family so that they wouldn't turn against us. Going ahead with this wedding wasn't the happily ever after I wanted, but I needed this. It was the only way not to be around my family's control and away from Emilio. I could tolerate seeing him occasionally, but constantly seeing the man you are in love with disregarding you was too much for me to bear.

Chicago's elite came piling in, greeting and congratulating us. Like Barbie and Ken, everyone complimented us on how picture-perfect we looked together—wearing a blush color mid-thigh high slit sheen satin dress pleated at the side with light boning at the waist giving the allusion of an hourglass body shape. The thin shoulder straps and draped neckline accentuated my chest in the most elegant way. Pio was dressed in a light grey designer suit with a matching blush color tie. His skin was as fair as mine, and his blonde hair was neatly cut and styled.

"Do you want something at the bar?" Pio asked me.

"Pinot, please," I smile in response.

I watched him approach the bartender and prayed that no one saw through this façade. Luca joins me as we both people watch.

"How is the soon-to-be bride?"

Smiling my hardest, I said, "Ready to walk down the aisle already."

Luca seemed happy for me, but why was it making me feel guilty? I stopped seeing Emilio, so there was no reason why guilt was eating at me whenever I saw my brother.

"I'm proud of you, B." Luca smiled.

"Not sure if I'll like Connecticut."

"If you want to stay in Chicago, just let me know. I'll make it happen."

I smile and then change the subject. "When do you find out about Aria and the baby?"

Luca shifted on his feet, "She's set to come in a few days."

"Are you nervous?"

"I try not to think about it."

Despite the circumstances, there was a spark between them. Sometimes, I'd catch them looking at one another with such intensity it made me jealous. Not that Pio wasn't good, but I couldn't help but question his genuine feelings when his father forced him to propose after dating for a month.

"Excuse me, I'll need to use the restroom."

Pushing my way through the crowd, I use the private restroom that is only for Pio and me. Needing a minute to breathe before breaking down, I quickly try to shut the door behind me, but someone comes plowing in.

"What the hell!" I shout as I move out of the way of the door.

Emilio walks right in and swiftly backs me into the door, locking it. We were face to face, and I felt the heat coming off his body as I stood in between his arms with his hands on the door. Our eyes locked, each displaying a sense of anger. My exposed open back against the cold wood door made me arch my chest forward. Emilio's line of vision drifted down to my breasts and was prompted forward. He looked as though he wanted to suck on them.

Barely an inch apart, "You're going through with it."

"I am."

"Because you want to?" Emilio asks, looking at me with fury eyes.

"He can give me what you can't." I held firm when I said the word, even though it killed me.

His eyes darkened while he stared deep into my eyes. Pushing off the door, he grabs my hand and makes me face the mirror above the sink counter.

"What are you doing?"

Emilio presses his body against mine as I face the mirror. I could feel his chest go up and down from his breathing and his heart practically beating outside his body as we locked eyes through the mirror. Placing his mouth by my ear, his hands grab my waist. One hand slides upward, touching my breast and making its way toward the thin strap of my dress, while the other hand slides downward the slit of my dress. Simultaneously, one hand slowly slides the strap off my shoulder, following the fabric fall off my skin, then grabbing my exposed breast, while the other hand reaches under my dress, making its way under my lace panty and then grabbing my pussy.

Leaning back on him, I gasp and try to get out of his grip. "No," I barely get out.

"Denying me, Bethany?" you could hear the lust pouring out of the sound of his voice into my ear.

"You can't have me." I manage to lean forward and off his body.

But he pulled me back in, "I can have you when I want."

Looking away, "Not anymore."

"Look at me and say it."

Forcing my head up, I look at him through the mirror. "We are done. It's what you wanted."

Pressing his body further into mine and wrapping his hands around my hips, he whispers into my ear, "The first night you gave yourself to me, you've been mine. That's not going to change."

He entered more than one finger inside of me as he twisted and pulled my nipple. I gasped for air and began panting. My heart was beating out my chest as his body was firmly against my back; his erection against my body was turning me on. But I can't give in no matter how much I want it. I've stayed strong for this long.

"Emilio—" his name panted out of my mouth.

Our eyes were locked in a stare, and he wasn't looking for me to change his mind or accept the fact I was putting my foot down on this being over. But the wetter I was getting inching toward an orgasm, the harder it was to resist him.

"This has to stop," I begged in a moan.

"You sure about that?" his voice was husky, and we both knew there was no going back now.

His thumb rubbed my clit, making my legs weak as his fingers continued to go in and out of me. My head fell back onto his chest in defeat. I place my hand on him, applying pressure, begging for him to enter further inside me.

Right as I was about to orgasm, there was a knock on the door. It shot me out of the moment when I heard who it was.

"Bethany, are you in there?" Pio's voice carried through the door.

"Shit," I let out the word in panic as I looked toward the door.

"Look at me," Emilio demanded without a flinch.

How was he being so calm? This was my rehearsal dinner. My brother, fiancé, and all of Chicago were outside those doors.

"Bethany?" Pio repeated.

"Tell him you're in here," Emilio said into my ear as his other hand grabbed my exposed breast.

"No way," I say in a low voice.

"Should I go open the door?" Emilio asked as he removed his hands from my body.

I knew he wasn't bluffing, so I shouted, "I'll be out in a minute."

"Is everything okay in there?" Pio asked.

A smirk crossed Emilio's face. He spun me around so I would face him. "Answer him."

As I replied to Pio, Emilio was unbuckling his pants. Shaking my head, I tried to push past him, but he stood firm. Pulling out his erection, he then grabs me by the thighs and lifts me onto the countertop.

"I have your wine," Pio went on.

"Okay," I reply. "I'll be out in a minute."

Emilio plunged inside of me, causing me to gasp loudly as he aggressively pounded his dick inside me. I cover my mouth with my hand. My legs wrapped around his waist, letting him take me as he wanted. At the moment, I didn't care if we were hiding in the bathroom, my fiancé was right outside the door, or my brother was nearby; I was devouring this moment for what it was. Panting, moaning, and skin-to-skin were echoing in the room.

"On my command," Emilio said.

Relentlessly fucking me, I wait for the okay even though I felt like my body was going to explode.

"Now, sweetheart."

We both climaxed keeping as quiet as possible. And when I finally caught my breath, I thought I'd feel some regret making it easy to walk away from this, but that wasn't the case. I don't think I could ever quit. Still with my legs wrapped around Emilio, while he was still inside me, I heard the door open.

Emilio never locked it.

Chapter 43

My heart raced as I quickly pulled down my dress and stood on my wobbly two feet, staring at the door. I was ready to explain the situation even though I'd be making it up. In slid a woman, tall with short blonde hair and red lips.

"What the fuck are you doing, Grace?" Emilio spat out as he zipped his pants.

"I should be asking you that," she smirked as she looked between us. "I saw Barbie's fiancé knocking; I figured something was going on that he wasn't supposed to see. So, I sent him on his way and bought whoever was in here some time. Unfortunately, I'm too nosy to just walk away."

Emilio nodded to her, "You both go first. I'll wait five minutes."

"You should go first," Grace replied, "Luca was asking for you."

It was obvious Emilio looked uncomfortable, and there were several reasons why. Grace is now aware of the situation, which only means this can now be used against him; my brother is looking for him, so if he doesn't have an alibi that makes sense, it will look suspicious; to top it off, this was poorly planned—how were we going to sneak out if we didn't know who was watching from the outside. Emilio walked out without a word while Grace stayed behind with me.

"Hey."

"Hi," I blushed from embarrassment.

She stood there looking at her watch.

I smile, holding my hands in front of me. "What you saw... um... it..."

"I saw nothing," Grace shot me a smile. "Ready to get back out there?"

Nodding my head, she then leads the way. Although no one in the room noticed I was gone, it felt as though everyone was eyeing me and whispering to one another about my scandalous ways.

"Bethany," Pio wraps his arm around my waist and pulls me in for a kiss on the cheek. "Your wine."

"Thank you." As we pulled apart, I saw Emilio standing with Alfie directly looking at me.

I want to say I felt dirty standing next to my fiancé after getting fucked in the bathroom by another man, but I wasn't. Not in the tiniest bit. Pio led me to a few people and introduced me to his side of the extended family from Connecticut. It felt like hours of smiling and pretending to be in love with the man I would marry in a few days. Emilio and I didn't speak the entire night, not that it was anything new, but each time he crossed my line of vision, I just wanted to run into his arms.

I was ordering another glass of wine. The amount I was drinking tonight, I'm surprised I wasn't falling all over the place.

"Macallan 1926 single malt." Looking beside me, I saw my brother ordering a drink. "Getting cold feet?" he asked.

"What makes you say that?" I shifted on my feet. Was I not smiling enough?

"Alfie mentioned you were hiding in the bathroom and sent Grace to check on you."

"Just feeling weird, that's all."

Luca gave me a look, "Pregnant?"

I laugh, "No!"

"Good," Luca laughed in return, "Mother can't handle a pregnancy out of wedlock."

We laughed, and, at that moment, I felt we had reconnected. Being the two youngest who grew up differently from our older siblings, it was important to me that Luca and I held our bond. Luca was in a good mood tonight, like he was his old self again.

"I want to stay in Chicago."

Luca nodded his head, "Figures."

I blush in panic, "Why?"

"Leaving your family isn't your thing. When you left and ran away, I didn't come for you because I wanted you to know what it was like without being around us. If it weren't for Emilio to convince me to bring you back, you might still be out there."

I shook my head, "Maybe not."

"Guess we will never know."

Emilio was right; Luca could never find out. It would damage our relationship, and Luca would kill Emilio no matter how much he wouldn't want to. Luca was big on trust, and if he found out his right-hand man was having an affair with his sister, it would be the ultimate betrayal. Maybe if there wasn't an arranged marriage and somehow, I got to expose a relationship with Emilio for Luca to approve, but it was too late. There was no going back. I made my bed, and now I will lay in it. I love my brother but won't give up on the one thing I can call mine. After all, Emilio is mine.

And I'll take this to the grave with me.

Epilogue

EMILIO

I knew better. This was wrong, but I couldn't stop, no matter how hard I tried. Every time I craved her touch, a part of me hated myself. She was my kryptonite. I walked the streets of Chicago a feared man, yet around her, I was powerless. For the past few years, I indulged in my selfishness, ignoring the fatality of my actions. We kept our affair a secret. No one had a clue—we made sure of it.

Pio was out of town, and I snuck into the house. As I walked through the back door, my phone pinged. It was a message from Alfie asking where I was. I sent a vague reply that I was handling something. He didn't reply.

As I entered further into the house, her cherry blossom scent lingered, which only made me more eager to devour her for the next few hours.

"You're late," her voice carried through the room I was approaching.

She laid in my favorite lingerie on a loveseat in the living room. We christened every inch of this house, but the loveseat was new, and I could tell she was looking to get it dirty by the look in her eyes.

"Traffic," I replied as I began to remove my jacket.

"You'll have to make up for it."

I watch her open her legs, exposing herself through the slit of her lace underwear. Her see-through bra exposed her nipple rings that hung there for décor. Wearing her snakeskin stilettos, she remained still as I undressed, building her anticipation. Once I was naked, I was on her immediately.

Usually, I preferred taking my time removing her clothes, but today was one of those days I just needed to be inside her right away. Bethany brought me a sense of reassurance that I was someone who could be loved. I'll never allow anyone to, but to know that I could be, meant something to me. Ripping off her lingerie, I immediately inserted myself inside her.

Watching her wrap her fingers around her nipples on her perfect breasts, the harder I pounded into her. Something about watching her touch herself made my dick throb. I could tell she was approaching her climax. Sliding my hand down to the inside of her thigh, she was soaked, and the closer my hand got to her pussy, the wetter it was. I push my thumb onto the top of her clit while thrusting upward, sending her into an orgasm as I watch her body explode and her scream in pleasure.

Taking a deep breath, I look into Bethany's eyes while still inside her. Without fail, every time I looked into them, they told me the same thing. I thought it would fade—that this was just a phase. But time hasn't changed a thing. She wanted me—my soul, mind, and body right down to the bones. Even knowing I couldn't fully give myself to her, she stayed. She didn't care as long as she had some part of me to hold on to. She deserved better than this and knew it, yet she stayed.

Before I could pull myself out of her, there was a change in her eyes from admiration to panic as she looked past my shoulder. I take a deep breath and look over my shoulder, expecting to see her husband. I planned for this moment to happen and knew exactly what to say to ensure this wouldn't blow up in Bethany's face. But when I saw who it was standing at the entrance, it was me this blew up on. Quickly turning onto my back, I grabbed a pillow to cover myself and sat beside Bethany, who lay frozen.

"What the fuck is going on!" The tone in Luca's voice was one that I'd never heard before.

Bethany snapped out of shock and sprang onto her knees, bowing in forgiveness as she pled, "Luca, please. Have mercy."

Made in the USA
Middletown, DE
10 April 2024